"This is where the police checked out, where they told me I was emotionally distraught over the death of my father."

Deirdre's voice caught. "They thought I ought to have my head examined."

"I'm not the police," Angel said.

The frightened woman gave a harsh laugh. "God, I hope not."

Again, she paused. Angel waited. A thing he was good at. One tended to develop certain skills when one was more than two hundred years old.

"Oh, what the hell," Deirdre finally said. "I suppose the first time somebody calls you a nutcase is always the worst, right? And it is why I came here, after all. I found evidence of a cult. A fire-demon cult."

Doyle flinched. "Those guys are the worst."

Angel™

Available from POCKET PULSE

The Essential Angel Posterbook

Available from POCKET BOOKS

ANGEL™

the summoned

Cameron Dokey

**An original novel based on the television series
created by Joss Whedon & David Greenwalt**

POCKET PULSE

New York   London   Toronto   Sydney   Singapore

Historian's Note: This story takes place during the first half of the first season of *Angel*.

This book is a work of fiction. Names, characters, places and incidents are products of the author's imagination or are used fictitiously. Any resemblance to actual events or locales or persons, living or dead, is entirely coincidental.

An *Original* Publication of POCKET BOOKS

 POCKET PULSE published by
Pocket Books, a division of Simon & Schuster, Inc.
1230 Avenue of the Americas, New York, NY 10020

I3DN. 0-7434-0700-8

First Pocket Books printing December 2001

10   9   8   7   6   5   4   3   2   1

POCKET PULSE and colophon are registered trademarks of
Simon & Schuster, Inc.

For information regarding special discounts for bulk purchases,
please contact Simon & Schuster Special Sales at 1-800-456-6798 or
business@simonandschuster.com

Printed in the U.S.A.

For Lisa and Micol,
with many thanks as always

CHAPTER ONE

It was night in the City of Angels. And the angels wept.

Their tears streamed over sidewalks. Filled up gutters. Stripped the heavy yellow smog from the air and hammered it down into the parched and dusty earth. All over the far-flung city, startled Angelenos lifted their heads. Cocked. Listening.

That sound. Oh, yes. Now they remembered. That was rain, wasn't it?

Rain. Water. Source and giver of life. Substance by which all things are renewed. Yet even in the midst of this rebirth, more than half a dozen unsuspecting people were fated to lose their lives in this rain, on this night.

Ellen Bradshaw was one of them. And not. Different from the others in one crucial respect.

She wasn't unsuspecting. She knew.

She stood on the corner of Third and La Brea,

shifting from one foot to another as she watched the traffic. Waiting for the light to change. Her normally curly red hair was plastered flat against her head. Water dripped from the end of her nose. She never noticed. Ellen Bradshaw had long since ceased to feel the rain.

Her right hand itched with the desire to ease upward so she could check her watch. Ellen resisted the temptation. She kept her leather-clad arms folded tightly across her chest, protecting the precious envelope her jacket concealed. Mailing it might well be her final act. But it would be her ticket to justice. And revenge.

Besides, what would be the point in checking her watch? She knew what time it was. Knew exactly how much time she had left.

Just barely enough.

It was 11:55 P.M., Pacific Daylight Time.

Ellen Bradshaw had just five more minutes to live.

The light changed and Ellen sprinted across the intersection, her boots splashing up arcs of water as she went. One of the motorists honked as a particularly large spray splashed onto the hood of his cherry-red Porsche. Ellen ignored him. She had more important things to think about than guys with delusions of Grand Prix grandeur. Besides, the driver was probably some old fart with a bad comb-over.

Against all odds, she found herself grinning as

she vaulted onto the sidewalk. *Is there any such thing as a good comb-over? As if.*

Ellen kept up the pace for one more block before turning off onto a sidestreet. She could see a high school, its big windows dark and vacant. Now that she was off the main street, the area around her was deserted. Not many sun worshipers chose to walk the rainy streets at 11:55 P.M.

But Ellen Bradshaw didn't have a choice. And if she'd ever worshiped anything other than her own needs, her own desires, she could no longer remember it.

Maybe that had been the problem, she thought as she slowed her pace to a brisk walk and sneaked a quick glance back over her shoulder. *There's nothing there, Ellen. Get a grip.* She was safe until straight up midnight. Or as safe as anyone could be on the streets of L.A.

Had she been the bait for her own trap? If she hadn't been so self-absorbed, would she have seen the truth? Acknowledged the horror crawling just beneath the surface of the beautiful gift that she'd been offered before it was too late?

No, not a gift, she thought as she crossed another street. She didn't look back again, but she couldn't shake the prickle, right between her shoulder blades. A gift was a thing that was given freely. And she knew now that nothing about what she had been offered—the dream she'd reached for so eagerly with both greedy hands—no part of it had ever been free.

Still, she'd never imagined the price would be so high.

She tightened her grip on the envelope, squeezing her arms against her chest.

The worst thing was that if she'd been content to let things stay the way they were, she'd still be safe. The thing that would kill her would be her own awakening. Her own good deed. *There has to be a name for that*, she thought as she paused for a moment to check her bearings. *Probably more than one*.

Poetic justice. Irony. Tough break, kid.

She swung left, onto a street whose sign had been knocked over in a traffic accident and never repaired. She could see it now, about two blocks up. On the left. There was a streetlight shining down on it, bright as a signal beacon, its beam alive with pelting drops of rain. A thing so ordinary and everyday nobody would look at it twice as an instrument of revenge.

A mailbox.

Ellen began to run again. *Hurry. Hurry. Hurry,* her heartbeats said. She was close now. So very close. To her goal. To the end.

Without warning, a figure appeared on the sidewalk in front of her, materializing out of the rainy darkness like a phantom. One that weighed in at about two hundred pounds, with hands the size of bone-in hams. With a cry Ellen skidded to a stop, her feet shooting out from under her on the rain-slick pavement. She went down, hard, her hands still clutching the envelope to her chest.

The figure took a step closer.

"Hey, lady. You got any change?" it asked.

Ellen made a strangled sound that might have been an attempt to laugh. This wasn't her doom. Not here. Not yet. In fact, she realized with a sudden flash of inspiration, it could be just the opposite. Her salvation.

All she had to do was to condemn this man to death.

Slowly, using her right arm to boost herself, Ellen got to her feet.

"You got any change?" the panhandler asked again.

Ellen plunged her right hand into her jacket pocket, searching for the thing she knew she'd left behind. The thing that wasn't supposed to be there. She also knew it *would* be there now, though she didn't understand how.

The Mark.

She'd known simply leaving it behind wasn't enough to get her off the hook. The only way to save her life was to get rid of it. Pass it to some unsuspecting, innocent bystander who wouldn't even know what he had until it was too late.

The summons for his own death.

Ellen had left the Mark in her apartment every day this week. Every single day since she'd received her sentence of death. Each day she'd done exactly the same thing, placing the Mark in the center of her desk. After that she'd followed her usual routine. Leaving the apartment. Walking to the bus stop.

And each and every day as she'd reached into her right pocket for her bus change, she'd found the Mark there instead. Like a token of faith, a pledge. Only one thing can part us, it seemed to say.

Death.

Yours, or somebody else's, Ellen. Take your pick.

She felt her seeking fingers close around it now. The Mark always felt warm. Why was that? Tonight it was so hot it all but burned her hand. The panhandler took a step forward, as if sensing she was about to offer something.

Do it, Ellen. Give it to him, a devilish voice in the back of her mind said.

Surely nobody would mourn if this guy didn't make it through the night. Nobody would notice if the sun rose tomorrow and he wasn't there. Life on the streets would claim one more nameless, faceless victim. The only one who'd know she'd murdered him would be Ellen herself.

That's not true, she realized suddenly. *They* would know. Because, come 12:01 A.M., she'd still be here.

They might even welcome her back with open

arms. Why not? Wouldn't she have proved she was still one of them? For all she knew, she'd be sitting even prettier than before. They'd probably give her a bonus, make her the poster child for a campaign to prove just how impossible it was to defy them and live to tell the tale.

All she had to do was to reach out her hand and hand over the Mark and she'd be home free. Safe. Back in the fold. On top of the world again. *Come on, Ellen,* the devil in her mind urged. *Just reach out, hand it over, and walk away.*

Ellen felt her right arm begin to tremble uncontrollably.

I can't do it, she thought.

How could she purchase a life she no longer wanted at the cost of another's? Oh, she wanted to live. No two ways about it. But she couldn't go back to the life they'd given her. The life she had to admit she'd chosen. She had to walk her new path. One she hadn't recognized until it was almost too late. But now that she had, it was impossible to turn aside.

Her eyes were open now. Even if all she saw was her own death staring her in the face, it was impossible to close them.

She released the Mark, shifted the envelope inside her jacket to her right arm, and reached her left hand into the other pocket. She came up with a handful of change and held it out.

"Here," she said. "It's all I've got. I'm sorry."

"Bitch!" the panhandler said as he snatched it away. "That won't even buy me a cup of coffee!"

Ellen felt an emotion she couldn't quite identify burst inside her chest. "Go to hell!" she shouted. This was the life she'd been afraid to take? The one she'd give her own for?

She sidestepped him, leaping into the street. Heard a wild laugh ring through the night and realized it was her own. *Hell,* she thought. She'd threatened him with it when it was so much more likely to be the place that *she* was going.

But not quite yet. First, she had to finish what she'd started.

She began to run toward the mailbox, full tilt down the center of the rain-slick street. On her right wrist her watch alarm was sending her a frantic signal.

Beep beep. Beep beep. Beep beep.

She'd set it to do that herself. The Ellen Bradshaw early-warning system.

It was 11:59 P.M. One minute to midnight. She had only one more minute to live.

Having delivered its message, her watch fell silent. Ellen could have sworn she felt time slow down as she continued down the street. The two blocks to the mailbox seemed to stretch out endlessly before her. The whole world went silent and still. Her own breaths, huffing in and out, were the only sounds in the universe. She could no longer hear the rain.

8

I'm never going to make it, she thought. She'd left it till too late. She was going to die for nothing. They were going to win.

"No!" The choked cry seemed to burst straight from her pounding heart. As if the sound of her own voice had broken some sort of evil spell, time resumed its normal course again. Ellen collided with the mailbox with a *clunk,* then wrapped her arms around it like it was a long-lost friend.

With desperate fingers she scrabbled for a hold on the handle as she reached inside her jacket for the envelope. She yanked the envelope out, pulled the door down, shoved the envelope into the dark and gaping maw of the mailbox. She released the door. It slammed shut with a *clang*. Ellen leaned her weight against it, pressing both palms flat, as if afraid the envelope might try to attempt an escape. Crawl back out and try to fly away.

Take that, you bastard.

She felt a spear of elation burst through her chest. It didn't matter what happened to her now. She had done it. Put in motion a sequence of events that, sooner or later, would take down the one who'd marked her. Condemned her to death. She hoped it would be sooner, but it really didn't make much difference.

Whenever he got to hell, he'd find her there, waiting for him.

Ellen pushed herself up from the mailbox, standing up straight, and heard her watch go off for the second time.

Beep beep. Beep beep. Beep beep.

Time's up. Time's up. Time's up.

It was midnight. The hour of her death.

Ellen spun around, setting her back against the mailbox. She wasn't quite sure why, the earlier prickle between her shoulder blades maybe, but she knew this was the direction from which her death would come. She was not about to let it stab her in the back. Ellen Bradshaw was going to meet her destiny head on. Face to face.

There was nothing there.

The sidewalk was completely empty. For the space of a dozen heartbeats, absolutely nothing happened. Then something seemed to flicker in the raindrops, taking form in the streetlight's glare. Ellen could have sworn the very air around her began to change. She could feel it thicken and grow hot, clogging as it moved in and out of her lungs. Clinging to her skin.

Her ears were filled with a strange sound, like bacon frying on a griddle. *It's the rain,* she realized suddenly. The drops were being sizzled from the air before they even reached the sidewalk.

And then, her death was there. Towering above her. Impossibly huge. Unbelievably horrible. Ellen took an involuntary step backward and felt the mailbox dig into her back. She didn't know what she'd expected, but it sure wasn't this.

It was a pillar of flame.

Inside the flame, an outline. Ellen could see arms. Legs. A head. A *face*.

Dear God, it's human, she thought. Or it had been once. Did this mean she could beg for mercy? Reason with it?

"Hello, Ellen," the thing before her said. Its voice the hiss of water over live coals. Ellen felt her gut clench. Her stomach muscles began to quiver uncontrollably. "I've come for you."

So much for reasoning with it. That left just one option. Ellen opened her mouth to beg.

That was when she saw them. Two eyes, staring at her from out of that fiery face. Clear as spring water in a polished glass. Hard as diamonds. Looking into them, Ellen felt her very heart shudder. She closed her mouth again.

There was no expression whatsoever in those eyes. They were flat and dead. More implacable than anything that lived on earth. Or ever would.

It would do no good to beg.

Before Ellen's mind could even conjure up the will to run, the thing of fire leaped straight for her. Enfolding her in an inferno embrace.

"Come to me, Ellen. Learn what happens to all those who would betray me."

Ellen had time to scream, just once, before fire

11

closed her throat. Seared her heart as it beat inside her chest.

Above her the streetlight exploded in a spray of shooting stars. High above the city, the angels looked down and dried their eyes.

They had no more tears left to shed.

CHAPTER TWO

Doyle was in the middle of a midnight Guinness run when the vision hit. As always, it wasn't precisely what a fellow would call pleasant.

For some reason Doyle had never understood, the Powers That Be, the supernatural do-gooders who'd tagged him as the designated visioner, were a lot like parents in some ways. Apparently, you had to feel bad to do good. The visions always involved headaches of the truly nauseating variety. Though this was a doozy, even by vision standards.

Doyle felt as if he'd taken a crowbar straight to the back of his head.

His knees gave way as the images rolled over him. Fear. Fire. Death. The usual, in fact. Except for the fire part. That was definitely a little different.

When Doyle got lucky, the visions were fairly

specific. Often, describing them aloud to his boss, Angel, the world's only vampire with a soul, allowed the team at Angel Investigations to pinpoint an exact location. Gave them a lead they could follow up on right away. That was everyone's first choice. Being able to move quickly gave them the greatest possibility for a positive outcome.

No such luck this time. This vision was all over the map. It was travelogue time inside Doyle's aching, pounding head.

He saw a young woman with red hair, screaming in agony. Her eyes, staring upward into the rain. Her neck arched, head straining back. He felt his own body bow, as if in sympathy, and could have sworn, for one split second, that he was looking through her eyes. Saw what she saw as a streetlight above her exploded in a burst of sparks like stars. In the next instant searing pain swept his entire body and the world went black.

But the vise that held his head in a grip of pain refused to let go. There was more. The vision wasn't over yet.

Out of the darkness a sea of faces seemed to swim toward him. All solemnly facing in the same direction. It reminded Doyle of a church congregation. Not that he'd seen one recently. But you didn't forget certain things. He was Irish, after all. Or his human half was.

As quickly as it had come, the image winked

out. Once more, darkness filled Doyle's head. In the dark, something flickered, then came into sharper focus. Tumbling end over end as if it had been tossed into the air. *A coin*, he thought. One he didn't think he'd seen before. The markings on it were strange to him.

Though, come to think of it, he'd yet to lay hands on one of those new Sacajawea dollars. Maybe it was one of them.

Down, down, down the coin tumbled. Straight toward Doyle's upturned face. It was going to hit him. He was sure of it. Just before it did, a pain as sharp and pure as any he'd ever known shot through his head. Right between the eyes like a red hot poker. His mind seemed to explode in a burst of fiery pain.

Fire, he thought. *The fire is the key.*

Then, as abruptly as it had struck, the pain receded. The vision was starting to pass. Doyle saw one last image, the outline of a human head. It reminded him of the way things looked right after somebody'd snapped a picture using a powerful flash. No details, just a bright outline superimposed against darkness. Was it part of the vision, or his return to the world?

Doyle came to flat on his back in the beverage aisle with the face of a woman bending over him and a six-pack of Guinness lying across his chest.

❖   ❖   ❖

Terri Miller hated L.A. No two ways about it. It might not have been so bad if she hadn't been so certain living here was going to be the answer to all her problems.

It was supposed to be easier to be anonymous in a big city, wasn't it? That's what she'd always heard. What she'd told herself anyway. With everybody afraid to make eye contact, studiously avoiding everybody else, surely the fact that nobody was looking at her anyway wouldn't be so obvious.

Fat chance.

Contrary to what Terri had hoped, the fact that people tended to overlook her altogether was even more obvious in L.A. than it had been in the small midwestern town where she'd grown up. And all because she hadn't reckoned with one thing. The fact that people in L.A. didn't make eye contact didn't mean they didn't look. They did. Every single minute of every single day.

Every place she went, Terri saw the same thing. To make herself feel better, she'd finally given it a name.

She called it the Drugstore Discovery Phenomenon.

The eyes of L.A. were never still. They were always searching the faces in the crowds around them. At the beach. On the street. In the mall. The grocery store. A quick glance out of the corners of their perfect makeup.

"Are you the one?" that glance seemed to say. "Will you be the next to be discovered, to make it to the top? Should I pay attention to you? Maybe even flash you a glimpse of my expensive dental work?

"Will you be *someone* someday?"

It was right after she'd named the phenomenon that Terri had realized the terrible truth: Nobody was looking at her. Nobody at all. It was like she was in some special no-man's land. Some twilight zone. A level of hell specifically reserved for people so boring they didn't even show up on the chart.

She'd given that a name, too. The Nobody Home Syndrome.

Nobody was looking because there was nothing there to see. It was obvious at fifty paces that Terri Miller was never going to be *someone*. She'd tried to tell herself this was a good thing. That it kept her safe, kept her from getting the wrong kinds of looks. How could you get the wrong kind when you didn't get any at all?

It hadn't worked.

Being a nobody wasn't the same thing as being stupid, as she'd long ago discovered to her cost. And it had hurt, more than she wanted to admit. Much, much more than she liked. Even so, not once did she ever consider going back home.

Going home would be to admit defeat, admit that her parents had been right all along. They were the first ones to tell her she was nothing, a nobody. First to proclaim she could never make it on her own.

In self-defense Terri had taken to staying in her apartment during the day, once her cleaning shift at the motel was over. She went out at night more and more. It had gotten so she lived pretty much her whole life after the sun went down. Fewer people to look right through her then. It meant she didn't see much of the famous So. Cal. sunshine, but Terri figured it was a small price to pay compared to constantly being reminded how unimportant she was.

Just call me Terri Miller, the Midnight Albino Shopper, she thought now as she pulled a grocery cart from its lineup and began to wheel it through the store. Lately, she'd begun to wonder if the fact that she was *so* unremarkable could be turned to her advantage. Maybe she could go on *Oprah* or something. Bill herself as the Woman Nobody Noticed.

She put a can of peaches in her cart, turned a corner, and proceeded down the baking aisle. It had taken her a while to get used to them, but her late-night trips to the supermarket had come to be about the only part of life Terri genuinely enjoyed. The wide, cool aisles were bright yet soothing all at the same time. She loved looking at all the different things there were to buy.

But the thing she liked best was that she didn't

have to worry about anything fitting right, or being in the latest *Vogue*. Nobody in the grocery store cared if she lingered over the jars of expensive designer pesto, maybe even put them in her cart and took them for a spin, before she exchanged them for the thing she could afford: canned spaghetti and meatballs.

Maybe she'd give herself a treat tonight, she thought as she added a chocolate cake mix to her shopping cart. She'd just been paid and had the day off tomorrow.

On impulse she suddenly put the cake mix back and reversed direction, heading toward the shelves filled with bottles of alcohol. Even after several months, she couldn't get used to being able to buy hard liquor in the grocery store. Not that that was what she wanted. But maybe a bottle of wine. If she could find one that would go down easy enough, maybe she could pretend she actually had something to celebrate. Forget, for a little while at least, just how dreary her small life was.

Way to go, Miller. Feel sorry for yourself. Now you're really accomplishing something. She turned into alcohol central, giving her cart a shove for extra emphasis.

There was a guy lying in the middle of the aisle.

For one horrified moment, Terri was afraid she'd knocked him down. Then she realized she couldn't have. She'd all but rolled the wheels of her cart right over his feet. She jerked the cart backward, releasing it as she hurried forward to bend over him.

"Omigod, are you all right?"

A pair of bleary blue eyes stared upward. Blinked twice. Then seemed to come into sharper focus.

"Yeah," the guy answered. "Thanks. I think so."

His voice had a lilt to it, even though he'd hardly spoken half a dozen words. Terri thought she recognized the sound of Ireland. That was when she noticed the six-pack of Guinness, flopped like a dead fish across his chest.

Uh-oh. He was probably just some drunk who'd had a few too many. He didn't smell like he'd been drinking, though. When Terri's dad had been on a binge, she could smell him clear across the room.

She lifted the six-pack from the guy's chest, set it in the aisle beside him, then helped him to his feet. He was on the small side, wiry, but she could feel that he was strong. He shook his head from side to side as if to clear it, the action making his dark hair flop across his forehead. Then, as if it had been too much, he swayed on his feet.

"Do you want me to call a doctor?" Terri asked anxiously, tightening her grip on his arm. Not that she knew one. But there was always 911.

"Not necessary," the guy replied. "It's just, I get

these . . . spells . . . sometimes. Come without warnin', like."

"Epileptic seizures?" Terri asked, then blushed. She could practically hear her mother's voice inside her head. *It's not polite to ask such personal questions. Not everyone wants to tell you their life story, Terri Nicole.*

"Something like that," the guy replied.

He didn't seem offended, and Terri felt herself relax, then tensed up again as she realized she was still holding on to his arm. She let go, stepped back quickly, and collided with her own shopping cart. A smile flitted across his face, making the blue eyes dazzling for a fraction of an instant.

"Easy now."

Terri realized her heart was pounding like a pile driver inside her chest. *He sees me,* she thought. For the first time in almost as long as she could remember, she had another person's undivided attention. Was the focus of a single pair of eyes.

"Well, thanks again for the help, but I've got to be goin'," the guy said. "I need to make a phone call."

He turned away, his six-pack of Guinness apparently forgotten, and began to make his way toward the far end of the aisle. He was going the wrong way if he wanted to get out quickly, but Terri didn't tell him. She was caught. Impaled on a spear of disappointment so sharp it made her want to cry out.

He was leaving. Going away. Terri could have sworn she felt her body slipping back into nothingness once more.

Then, as she watched, the guy stopped short. Turned to look back over his shoulder, hesitating a moment. Finally he began to retrace his steps. He was coming back toward her. His eyes once more upon her. Terri wondered if her heart would simply explode.

"Look, don't get me wrong or nothin'," the guy said as he approached her. Again, she heard the Irish in his voice. "I appreciate your help, and all. But you should really be more careful about strangers. You don't know me. I could be anyone."

His eyes flicked past her, to focus on something she couldn't see. "What if I'd been running some scam? Had a partner? We could have had your purse by now."

Horrified, Terri spun around. Her purse was right where she'd left it, in the front of the cart. The same place she'd ridden, holding on to her mother's purse, when she was a child. She could feel a hot blush begin to creep its way slowly up her neck.

He's right, she thought. She'd been in such a hurry to make sure he was all right, she'd completely abandoned the key to all her worldly possessions. She knew why she'd held his attention for so long now. He'd probably never seen anybody quite so stupid.

"I'm sorry," she choked out as she turned back to face him. "I didn't think. I—"

"See, that's just the thing," he said, his voice urgent with an emotion she could hear but not identify. "You can't afford not to think in a place like L.A. You have to stay on your guard. All the time."

She nodded her head, not trusting herself to speak. If she tried to say anything, she was afraid she'd start to cry. Why couldn't being nothing mean she felt nothing, too? She'd wished for it often enough. But, as always, it seemed her wish would not be granted. Not here. Not tonight.

An expression that looked like regret passed across his face. "Come on," he said. "Don't take it so hard. I'm grateful you tried to help, really I am. I'm tryin' to do you a favor for the future is all." He reached out. For one horrified moment Terri thought he meant to pat her on the head, the way he would a dog.

Almost before she realized she'd done it, Terri jerked back, scraping her heels painfully against the front of the shopping cart.

"Don't touch me," she choked out. She could hear her own voice, thick with tears, and hated herself for it. Were there no limits to the ways in which she could make a fool of herself? Apparently not.

She cleared her throat. "Thanks for the free advice," she said, her voice stronger the second time around. "Feel free to take a hike any time now."

"All right," he said. He dropped his arm back to his side. "That's good. That's just fine." This time he went the right direction, brushing past her. She didn't turn to watch him go.

Instead, she stood in the aisle, counting to a hundred to steady herself. Then she did it a second time. Only when she felt sure he must be gone did she turn and grope for her purse, closing trembling fingers around it, her desire to celebrate completely forgotten.

Eyes all but blind with tears, Terri Miller fled from the grocery store.

You sure as hell blew that one, Boyo, Doyle thought to himself. He shouldn't have been so hard on that girl, whoever she was. She'd only been trying to help. *Had* helped, in fact. He'd said thank you. The smart move would have been to leave it at that and get on with it. But Doyle had never been very good at leaving well enough alone.

Besides, something about her had pulled at him. A thing that had compelled him to try and warn her. Something that seemed to tell him she'd already been hurt more than enough. That she had no one to help or protect her. That she was all alone.

24

Or maybe it had been even simpler, and much more selfish. He didn't want her on his conscience. *I wonder if this is how Angel feels?* he thought. Though, now that he thought about it, he had to doubt it. There was really no comparing anything he might feel to what Angel felt. No way a half human/half demon messenger boy for the Powers That Be *could* compare to a more-than-two-hundred-year-old vampire. Particularly one that came complete with a soul.

A situation which was actually just fine by the likes of one Francis Doyle. There were some things to which a guy simply shouldn't aspire, after all.

Doyle reached the grocery store's big glass doors, paused a moment while they slid open, then moved through them, his eyes searching for the nearest pay phone. There it was, out in the open, but at least the rain had stopped.

It must have been the vision that had prompted him to try and warn the girl, he decided as he loped toward the phone. The images had departed. But they'd left a sense of urgency behind. An overwhelming impulse he couldn't ignore: Protect innocent things from harm.

When he'd first come to, he'd felt a surge of relief, certain it was the girl in the vision bending over him. It had taken only a couple of seconds to realize he was wrong. The girl in the vision had red hair. The face that had bent over him with such concern had hair of a color that could charitably be called mousy brown.

Everything about her had reminded him of a mouse, in fact. High forehead, small pointed nose. A mouth that was just a tad too wide; a chin that was too small. Not an ugly face, precisely. Just not a very memorable one.

He forgot about it as he reached the pay phone.

Ordinarily, he'd have alerted Angel on his cell. But the cell phone of Cordelia Chase—Doyle's co-worker and Angel Investigations' self-proclaimed office manager—was on the fritz. This had freaked her so completely that Doyle had finally broken down and loaned her his own.

Though she actually spent most of her time hanging out at the office making truly terrible coffee, and informing Angel at every opportunity that she was the one who was keeping him organized, Cordy had never forgotten her reason for coming to L.A. in the first place: her aspirations of being a star. The fact that she was willing to put in a few hours helping an old friend from her high school days in nearby Sunnydale atone for a hundred years of bloodsucking mayhem didn't mean she'd stopped waiting for her big Hollywood break to come.

The thought that *the call* might come and she wouldn't be able to get it had all but made her certifiable. She'd whined about it nonstop, finally making Angel and Doyle certifiable as well. When Angel had retreated to his downstairs quarters, Doyle had felt he'd had no choice but to give up his own phone. It was self-defense, after all.

Though he'd been careful not to mention a thing Cordelia had apparently overlooked. Her big call to stardom was unlikely to come through on somebody else's cell phone.

I must be going soft in the head, Doyle thought now. He was the one who got the visions, wasn't he? He was the direct link with the Powers That Be. He got the visions, Angel atoned. That was the setup. The way things were supposed to go. He'd just had a vision that was truly off the charts. But could he reach Angel quickly, now that every second counted? He could not.

Doyle dug one hand into a pocket, producing his last quarter like a magician performing his most famous trick, and turned to the pay phone.

"What the bleedin' hell?"

Terri Miller stood in the parking lot, fumbling for her car keys. Unable to put the incident with the guy in the grocery store from her mind. Not the warning he'd given, though that had made her feel stupid enough. No, the thing that had her stomach roiling in humiliation, her hands shaking so that she could hardly unzip her purse, was what had happened before.

He'd looked at her. *Seen* her. Yanked her back into the world of human contact. And in so doing, he'd blown her whole carefully constructed existence straight to kingdom come. By his gaze, he'd drawn hopes she'd almost forgotten she had out of hiding. Then he'd turned and walked away, leaving them to freeze out in the cold.

Even then that wasn't the worst. The worst part was that he'd never even realized what he'd done.

Finally Terri managed to make the zipper move along its track, plunged her hand into the depths of her purse, searching for her car keys. Somehow, they never stayed in their special little compartment. Why was it she could never find them?

I'll tell you why, her mind said, the answer swift and brutal as a kick to the stomach. *Because you're stupid and worthless. A whole new definition for the phrase "lost cause."*

How on earth could she have convinced herself she was making it here? Doing all right on her own? All it had taken was one look from a stranger for her to know the truth.

She was miserable. Desperately alone. And she was a liar. Of the worst kind. Not one who lied to other people. One who lied to herself. She'd told herself she had a life, even if it wasn't the one that she'd envisioned.

The truth was, she had nothing. *Was* nothing. Absolutely nothing at all.

Her fingers located the car keys, closing around the tiny stuffed teddy bear that dangled from the end of her keychain. She'd won it at a carnival, years ago. It was one of the few mementos she'd brought from home. She yanked the keychain free of her bag.

"Terri?" said a hoarse voice.

With a startled cry Terri spun around. The car keys flew from her suddenly numb fingers.

"Septimus," she choked out.

"I'm sorry, Terri. I'm sorry," the guy named Septimus said. He twisted his hands together, over and over.

"It's all right, Septimus," Terri said, trying to ignore the way her heartbeats still thundered in her ears. "You just startled me, that's all." She'd thought the evening couldn't get much worse. Now she realized she'd been wrong.

Septimus lived on the streets. Terri didn't know exactly where. All she knew was that he had a home base somewhere near her apartment. She'd met him not long after she'd moved to L.A. All the other tenants in her building avoided him like the plague. Terri wasn't quite sure why she felt drawn to help him. She thought it was because she'd seen Mr. Taylor, the building super, get rough with him just for hanging around.

ANGEL

"Did you get them?" Septimus asked now. His voice was eager. He'd stopped wringing his hands and thrust them deep into the pockets of his camouflage overcoat.

Instantly a wave of guilt washed over Terri. She'd been so upset by her encounter with the guy in the store, she'd forgotten all about the items she usually got for Septimus. Sometimes it was staples like bread or cheese. But the thing he really loved was animal crackers. The kind in the little cardboard box with the string handle.

"I'm sorry, Septimus," she said. "I didn't get them. I—I didn't feel well so I—" She broke off, the excuse sticking in her throat. *Selfish, self-indulgent,* her mind accused. He's so much worse off than you are, yet you put yourself first. You forgot all about him.

Septimus took a step back, as if he'd seen something in Terri's face that frightened him. "That's okay, Terri," he said. He began to edge away. "Maybe tomorrow night?"

"Sure, Septimus," Terri said. "Maybe tomorrow." She watched as he cut between the rows of cars, weaving his way out of the parking lot. Where would he go now? she wondered. Would he walk the streets, looking for loose change? Would he get anything to eat tonight? A sense of failure greater than any she'd ever known washed over Terri.

I don't want to do this anymore, she thought. Didn't want to keep fooling herself about the fact that she was making it here. That she was doing well enough to help someone. How could she help Septimus when she couldn't even help herself?

"Excuse me," a new voice said. "But are these yours?"

Terri stiffened, instinctively turning away. Just what she needed. Another guy to witness yet another humiliating moment. Though, now that she thought about, she supposed it did make sense. She *was* nobody. So of course she had nowhere to run. Nowhere to hide.

"Here. Why don't you let me?" the guy went on.

Terri felt hands on her shoulders, felt herself being gently moved aside. A moment later she heard the squeak her key always made as it turned in the lock.

"Okay," he said. "It's open now. You might want to squirt a little WD-40 into that lock. It'd take care of that squeak."

As if from a great distance, Terri heard her own voice.

"WD-40?"

In response she heard the last sound she expected. A quick and genuine laugh.

"You're kidding right?"

Terri was so startled, she turned around. Facing her was one of the best-looking guys she'd ever seen. The kind of looks that, no matter where she lived in the future, would always remind her of her time in Southern California.

Blond hair made light by the sun. Chiseled face tanned, made darker. Even in the dim light of the parking lot, she could see that his eyes were blue. The same color as the ocean. A poster boy for a modern-day Prince Charming. One wearing a lightweight sportscoat, a white button-down shirt, and a pair of jeans that fit him like a second skin. He jingled her greasy car keys in one hand.

"You never heard of WD-40? Guaranteed to cure anything that squeaks. Scout's honor. Try a couple squirts in that lock, and you'll see what I mean." Without warning, he leaned a little closer, as if trying to get a better look at her. "Hey, are you okay?" he asked, his voice softening. "You look a little—"

"I know what I look like," Terri rasped out in a voice that made her own throat sore. "I don't need you to tell me. I need you to leave me alone. Give me my car keys."

She was surprised to see something that looked like hurt flicker across his face, in the depths of his blue, blue eyes.

"Okay," he said as he handed over the keys. "But you got me wrong, you know. I didn't mean that. All I meant was—"

He paused, as if weighing his next words carefully. "I understand how easy it is to get lost in a place like L.A."

Terri was never certain why she answered. It wasn't like her to sass anybody. Her parents had made sure of that. Maybe it was that she was so sure she had nothing left to lose.

"Oh, sure you do," she said. "You don't know a damn thing about it. A guy who—" *Looks like you. Could have anyone he wanted.*

Suddenly horrified by what she'd almost blurted out, Terri shut her mouth with a snap. This time she recognized the expression that flashed at the back of his eyes. It was anger.

"Go on, say it," he rapped out. "A guy who looks like me. I should have known you were just like all the others. A brainless sheep. You think looking like this gives me a charmed life, don't you? Well, you can guess again. But you know what? I don't have to care about what people like you think. Not anymore. Because now I have—"

"I'm sorry—" Terri interrupted.

They broke off, staring at each other.

"No, really, I'm sorry," Terri said again. She hated the thought that she'd hurt him, misunderstood him. Failed to see him, just as others did her. "I've had a horrible day, and I—"

"I can help," he broke in.

Terri felt her heart leap even as her brain offered its denial. "I don't think so."

"No, really," he insisted. "I can."

Somehow, Terri managed a laugh. She'd been a total jerk, and he was offering to help. "I don't know why you'd want to."

"Because I meant it," he said. "I *do* know how you feel. Lost. Alone. Like no one understands you, or even sees you. The real you."

Terri felt her head begin to spin. That was it. That was it, exactly.

"How can you know?" she whispered.

He gave her a smile that was dazzling in its brightness. As if she were a prize pupil who'd just asked the million-dollar question.

"Because I used to feel the same way," he said. "But I found something that made it better. That gave me the life I wanted. I can help you find it, if you'll let me."

This can't be happening, Terri thought. *It has to be a dream.* Guys who looked like Prince Charming didn't walk up to girls like her and say things like this. They didn't walk up to girls like her at all.

"How?"

He gave her a different smile this time. One that made him look like a kid with a new toy he wanted to show off.

"Let's back up a minute and do this right," he said. "My name's Andy, what's yours?"

"Terri."

"Terri," he repeated softly, as if committing it

to memory. "It's nice to know you." Then his energy revved, getting to the heart of the matter. "So—about what we were talking about a minute ago—"

At the sound of a beeper going off, they both jumped. Andy's hand went to his inside jacket pocket in a gesture so unerring Terri knew this had to happen all the time. He pulled the beeper out, silenced it, then checked the number. As he did so, all the exuberance seemed to drain from his face, leaving something darker, more intent behind.

"I'm sorry," he said. "I have to answer this. I'm on call. I have to go." He returned the beeper to his pocket and looked around the parking lot, as if just now remembering where they were. "Damn," he muttered.

Terri battled back her rising disappointment. She'd been so close. "What is it?" she asked.

"My car's in the shop. Can you believe I totally forgot I walked here? Who knows how long it'll take me to get a cab this time of night."

Terri had a realization so astounding she almost dropped her keys again. He needed her.

"Let me take you," she offered.

Andy looked surprised. Then, amazingly, touched. "You'd do that?" he asked.

"Sure," Terri said. "Why not?"

But even to her own ears her voice sounded funny. Bright with a confidence she didn't quite feel. Wasn't this the kind of thing the guy in the grocery store had just warned her about? Helping a total stranger. Aside from his name, she knew absolutely nothing about this guy.

That's not true, Terri realized suddenly. She did know one thing more. She knew the way he made her feel. Good. Important. Real. Alive. And that had just been standing in the grocery-store parking lot. If he could really do what he claimed, tell her how to have the life she'd always wanted, who was to say what she might feel?

I don't care if it's risky, she thought. Wasn't that what life was supposed to be about? Taking risks?

"You helped me. The least I can do is return the favor," she said.

"But it's clear across town," Andy protested.

"That doesn't matter," Terri said firmly. Somehow, she had to convince him. She couldn't just let him walk away. She wanted what he'd offered. A chance at a new life.

"I gotta admit, it sure would help," Andy said. "Even if you just took me part way."

Terri felt a rush of relief and elation. "As far as you like."

Andy nodded. "Okay. But I accept on one condition. That we continue our conversation along the way."

Terri felt her heart begin to sing.

"I'd like that," she said.

*　　*　　*

Doyle stared at the phone booth in disbelief. Talk about out of touch. Since when did it cost thirty-five cents to make one lousy phone call?

He flipped open the pay phone's coin slot. Nothing. And the quarter he was waving uselessly in the air was all the change he had. *Now what?* Doyle wondered. Place a collect call to his own place of employment? He could head back into the store and waste precious minutes trying to convince one of the checkers to make change. Or he could just bag the phone thing entirely and head for the office.

As he stood hesitating, a car pulled out of the parking lot. A battered green Dodge Dart. As it passed beneath the glow of a nearby streetlight, Doyle thought he recognized the girl behind the wheel as the one who'd tried to help him. He lifted a hand to flag her down.

In the next instant he dropped his arm back to his side. *Must have been a trick of the light,* he thought.

It couldn't be the same girl. There had been something about her that had all but screamed she was alone. But there was someone in the passenger seat of the old Dart. A guy. The two were deep in conversation, just like old pals. In the sudden illumination of the streetlight, the girl's face was open, smiling.

Definitely not the same girl, Doyle thought.

The car pulled from the lot, out from under

the streetlight, plunging the interior into darkness. It turned and sped away. Doyle put the incident from his mind.

He had to get to Angel before it was too late. Assuming it wasn't already.

Turning in the opposite direction from the one in which the car had gone, Doyle began to run.

CHAPTER THREE

In a darkened apartment a telephone rang. Once. Twice. A bedside light snapped on. Slim, capable fingers reached unerringly for the pen that sat on the nightstand. Uncapped it, then set the top down and picked up the pad of paper that sat beside the phone. Before the third ring had ended, the connection was open.

"Lockley."

"I'm sorry to bother you, Detective," the caller said. "But a . . . certain type of incident . . . has occurred again. You had requested to be kept informed."

The hand holding the pen jerked, making a thick black line across the sheet of blank white paper. Detective Kate Lockley took a breath. Sat up a little straighter in bed. Gripped the pen a little more tightly.

"Yes, I see," she said. "Thank you for calling. Please go on."

She listened for several moments, making swift, terse notations as the caller spoke. Only when her informant had finished speaking did she ask a question.

"Officers called to the scene?"

Her frown grew deeper as she listened to the response.

"I see," she said. "No, no more questions. Thank you for your call."

She sat still for a moment, just barely aware that her phone had begun to emit a dial tone. She stared into space, the pen moving in an unconscious movement up and down across the paper, creating an angry, jagged line. Only when the phone began to beep, protesting her still-open connection, did she move, hitting the Off button and cradling the receiver.

"Damn," she swore.

With swift, deliberate motions, Kate re-capped the pen, tore her notes from the pad, then set pen and pad back on the nightstand, ready for the next phone call. Throwing back the covers, she got out of bed, heading for the shower. She gave the cold-water knob a vicious twist, turning the spray on full force. Then she shrugged out of her nightgown and stepped beneath the freezing water.

✳   ✳   ✳

In an office in a high-rise tower of steel and glass, a second telephone rang on a desk the color of ebony, polished to a luster deep enough to reflect the young man seated behind it. In spite of the fact that it was quite literally the middle of the night, he was impeccably dressed in a slate-gray business suit accented by a tie the deep maroon of ox blood.

He picked up the phone halfway through the fourth ring.

"Yes," he said. A statement, not a question.

The caller spoke. The young man listened, his fingers toying with a slim silver pen. Tapping it against a notepad embossed across the top in bold black letters.

Wolfram & Hart.

But the young man took no notes. He never even uncapped the pen. He'd been trained well, and he'd paid attention.

No notes, no paper trail.

"I see," he said after a few moments. "I'm sure the partners will be pleased to know that this matter has been concluded so satisfactorily. I can assure them we're back on track then?"

He listened for another moment, his expression pleased. "And the other situation we discussed?"

At the response he flashed a quick and feral grin. "Excellent," he said. "I trust you'll keep me informed." Another statement. He didn't wait for an answer. Instead he reached out and severed the connection.

He placed the receiver back in its cradle, the pen in the desk's top drawer. He aligned the pad in the very center of the desk. Then he sat back, his fingers steepled beneath his chin, surveying his small domain.

Everything was in order. In its proper place. On track. Only when he'd assured himself of that did he permit himself one small luxury.

He began to laugh.

"Well, this is a zoo," Angel said, his tone just short of sour.

It was about an hour after Doyle's vision, approximately 1:00 A.M. Though the Powers That Be hadn't been thoughtful enough to provide any location clues to follow up on, the television had. Doyle had arrived at the office to find Angel watching a late-breaking news report about a fire near the La Brea Tar Pits.

"What have you got?" he'd asked as an out-of-breath Doyle had staggered in through the door.

"Fire" was all that Doyle had said.

As a result, the two were standing on the outskirts of what was literally L.A.'s hottest crime scene. Or had been. The fire was out now, had been since before they'd arrived. But that hadn't diminished the number of people still on the scene. Police. Spectators. Press. The place was a definite happening.

It was also an emormous mess.

One of the fire trucks called to the scene had lost control as it came around the corner, skidding half a block on the rain-slick street. It had rammed a mailbox right in the center of the action, scattering its contents in every direction, forcing the cops to try and retrieve mail at the same time they sought to preserve the sanctity of their crime scene. Hardly their favorite sort of multitasking.

As Angel and Doyle watched, a figure standing just outside the yellow tape made a sudden lunge, snatched a large, white envelope from the pavement, stuffed it inside his camouflage overcoat, then scuttled away. A nearby cop yelled at him to stop, cursing and aiming a kick in his general direction when his directive failed.

Then he turned around quickly, as if suddenly realizing that his actions could have been caught on tape. In the next moment he vanished into the knot of policemen clustered in the vicinity of the fallen mailbox. Anonymity in action.

Doyle cocked an eyebrow at Angel. "And what sort of animal would that be?" he asked.

Angel's keen eyes continued to survey the site as he answered, "I think it's called a jackass."

He gave a jerk with his head, signaling his intention to sidle to the left. Doyle followed without further comment. One of the things Angel liked best about Doyle was the way he didn't need everything spelled out for him. He didn't require an explanation for every little thing, the way Cordelia sometimes did. And, though Doyle could be quite gregarious himself at times, he didn't regularly require Angel to chat.

Angel maneuvered around a group of teenagers, eagerly watching the scene and talking animatedly among themselves.

"You should have seen it, man," one of them said. "It was like—" He made an explosive sound, accompanied by expansive hand gestures. "And that was just the very end."

"Cool," one of his companions commented.

Angel shook his head.

No wonder he sometimes felt less than one hundred percent sure about the whole trying to get in touch with the living aspect of his current arrangement. There were some things about the living he just didn't get.

Like, say, for instance, their fascination with and insistence on glamorizing death. Though Angel supposed he did have a pretty unique perspective on the matter, considering the fact that he was, himself, officially dead.

If there'd been a scene like this when he'd been alive, a little more than two hundred years ago now, chances were good his response would have been much the same as these contemporary young people, he had to admit. Which only went to show why getting all warm and fuzzy about the living now was sometimes such a struggle. Even when he'd been alive, he hadn't exactly been Mr. Sensitive.

He continued his progress, making for the edge of the crowd closest to the crime scene.

"We taking the scenic route, or what?" Doyle inquired.

That was another thing Angel appreciated—Doyle's sense of humor. In moderation, of course.

"I want a closer look."

"Good luck," Doyle said.

He had a point. There were still an awful lot of bodies between them and whatever had happened here. Still, now that there weren't quite so many other spectators in his way, Angel could see enough to get the gist.

The sidewalk in front of the fallen mailbox looked like someone had hit it with an enormous blowtorch. It was black and scorched, its surface pitted. Angel didn't know for sure just how much heat it took to make a cement sidewalk look like that. But he had to figure it was somewhere in the realm of more than he'd ever want to mess with.

"Check that out," Doyle said quietly, with a lift of his chin.

Above the mailbox was a burned-out streetlight, its big bulb completely shattered. Shards of glass littered the ground beneath.

"You think that's the one from your vision?" Angel inquired.

"Could be," Doyle said.

Which would put them in the right place at what was very definitely the wrong time. A thing that very definitely bothered him. In the center of the blackened sidewalk lay a police tarp. So far nobody was saying what it covered, but Angel figured he could make an educated guess: something dead.

"We're too late," Doyle said.

"Looks that way," Angel agreed. No sense in pulling punches.

"Angel, man, I'm sorry. Maybe if I'd gotten to you sooner . . ."

"I don't think so," Angel interrupted. "Whatever happened here was over by the time your vision was."

A thing that didn't make much sense. The visions were supposed to enable him to intervene for the cause of good, right? Even for someone with Angel's unique perspective and abilities, it was pretty hard to do an intervention on someone who was already dead, most likely burned to a crisp.

Without warning, a blindingly bright light came on not far from where Doyle and Angel stood. One of the TV reporters was getting ready to do a stand-up. In the sudden glare of the light, Angel thought he saw a familiar figure, swiftly stepping away from the crime scene, out of the light's range.

Kate Lockley.

"Hey," Doyle said. "Isn't that—"

"Yep," Angel answered.

The question was, what was Kate doing here? It obviously wasn't her case, nor was she even assigned to it. She was on the wrong side of the crime-scene tape. Cops didn't just randomly show up at crime scenes, even major ones. They already had too much to do, and they definitely knew better than to get in the way. So why was Kate prowling around, obviously anxious not to be observed? What was her interest?

Angel lost sight of Kate as the woman reporter began to speak.

"Citizens of Los Angeles are locking their doors in fear again tonight," she announced, her tone and expression signaling viewers that she was deadly serious about this. Just how deadly was the thing Angel had a feeling it was now his job to find out.

"Though police have yet to officially confirm this, inside sources tell us the Krispy Kritter Killer has just claimed another victim."

Angel felt something ugly roil in the pit of his stomach. He'd heard about the killer the press had given the macabre nickname Krispy Kritter, based on his preferred modus operandi of burning victims to death. Who in L.A. hadn't? There'd been nearly a dozen victims in the last few months alone. A terrifyingly impressive body count by anybody's standards.

Equally disturbing was the fact that, as far the police could tell, or were saying anyway, there was absolutely nothing to link the victims together. Nothing except the manner of their deaths.

They were different races, ages, genders. They came from all over L.A. The Krispy Kritter was everybody's worst nightmare. A serial killer whose victims could be anyone, come from anywhere. Who claimed them with a method that destroyed evidence. Who defied profiling by breaking all the rules.

To say that L.A.'s finest were not happy campers was an understatement.

But, horrifying as the crimes were, there'd been nothing to link them to anything other than some terrible impulse locked deep within some malformed human heart and brain. Nothing to show that the situation required Angel's intervention, though it certainly had his attention.

Not until tonight. When Doyle's vision had brought them here too late.

"I've seen enough," Angel said abruptly. "Let's get out of here."

He had it. The envelope with the pretty stamps on it. His father would probably be furious if he knew. He'd say that it was stealing. But Septimus knew better. He hadn't taken it from anybody, or even from a mailbox. He'd found it, lying on the ground. The rule was finders keepers, losers weepers.

Everybody knows that, he thought.

It hadn't even been inside that tape the police had stretched out everywhere, like a thick yellow spiderweb. Septimus had made sure of that. The envelope had been resting right outside. He knew better than to go on the wrong side of the yellow tape. He'd seen a lot of it, in his time. He even knew what it said: POLICE LINE DO NOT CROSS.

Besides, it wasn't like he was going to keep the envelope forever. He just wanted to borrow it for a while. To dry it out, and look at the pretty stamps. They had pictures of animals on them. Septimus liked animals. He liked them a lot. Even more, he knew that Terri did, too. Maybe, if he showed her the stamps, she'd start to feel better. She wouldn't look so sad and hurt, the way she had tonight.

He wanted to make Terri feel better. She was the only person who'd cared about him, even a little, in a long, long time.

Clutching the envelope to his chest, Septimus Stephens shuffled through the dark L.A. streets, heading for the alley he currently called home.

CHAPTER FOUR

Hours passed. The human inhabitants of the City of Angels tossed and turned in fitful sleep, those who slept at all, as the clouds parted and the stars wheeled above. Slowly, inexorably, it began to happen. That thing that always happened. That thing no one could ever stop, or even control.

Night gave way to day. Dark to light. Yesterday to the today that had once been tomorrow. If you still had a life, it went on.

In a stylish apartment on the beach in Malibu, a young woman stood at a window. Her brown eyes stared intently out but were focused entirely inward. She saw nothing of the waves dashing themselves against the beach in the chill, gray dawn.

Without warning, a loud buzzing filled the room. She jumped, one hand coming up in a defensive gesture, as she whirled around. In the next moment she strode forward, shaking her head as if at her own stupidity. Walking purposefully into the bedroom, she turned off her alarm. Her bed was still made. She hadn't slept in it at all.

The time was 6:00 A.M. Pacific Daylight Time.

On autopilot, she went into her morning routine. Making coffee in a French press, trying not to notice the fact that her knuckles turned white with tension as she pressed the plunger down. Armed with a cup of thick, black liquid, she returned to the living room and sat behind the desk stationed near the window.

No more putting things off. It's showtime.

On the surface of the desk, a telephone. A photograph of a man in an elegant silver frame. And one manila file folder. On a label across the tab at the top, in black capital letters, were two words. A proper name.

The woman took a bracing sip of coffee, set the cup down, and pulled the folder toward her. She opened it, and found herself staring into the eyes of the woman identified on the label.

Ellen Bradshaw.

The photograph had caught Ellen walking down the street, glancing back over her shoulder as if she feared that she was being followed. Her expression was shuttered, furtive, but her eyes were wide and frightened. Even at a distance the camera had caught the dark circles beneath them, curved like half-moon bruises. Her red hair was wild about her head. Her right hand was plunged into her jacket pocket.

The woman at the desk sat perfectly still, staring at the photograph, her coffee growing cold, forgotten.

Then, without warning, she moved, her motions jerky and abrupt. She closed the folder with a soft *slap* and yanked open the right desk drawer. Her fingers scrabbled until they located the objects she desired. Two thick-tipped felt pens. One red. One black.

After uncapping the black pen, she drew a line across the top of Ellen's folder. With the red she wrote the word DECEASED in capital letters diagonally across the front. Then she highlighted the label in red as well. Re-capped the pens; put them away. For all the world as if she were completing a school assignment.

Opening the large bottom drawer of the desk, she slipped Ellen Bradshaw's folder into the first of a set of hanging files and slammed the drawer shut, the sound echoing like a gunshot in the silent apartment.

What now?

But she'd already answered her own question. As if of its own volition, her right hand reached for the photograph on the desk in front of her.

The man in the photograph looked to be in his

early sixties. The resemblance between him and the woman at the desk was strong. They both had the same alert, dark gaze. The same pointed chin that somehow only served to strengthen the never-say-die jawline.

Across the photograph was an inscription, written in a bold, flowing hand: *For Deirdre. So I'll always be there to keep an eye on you.*

She blinked rapidly against an unexpected flush of tears. *Oh, Dad,* she thought.

The phone rang, shrill and loud. Deirdre started, her motion toppling the photo facedown. She snatched the phone up, pressing the receiver to her ear.

"Arensen."

"Deirdre? It's Kate," said the voice on the other end of the phone. "I'm sorry to call so early, but I thought you'd want to know as soon as possible. It's confirmed. There's been another one."

For the first time all night the woman named Deirdre Arensen closed her eyes.

"Yes," she said. "I know."

"Find anything?" Doyle asked.

Angel made a sound of frustration and pushed back from his book-piled kitchen table.

"Not unless you want to count a couple of killer dust bunnies."

It was not quite nine o'clock, almost time for Cordelia to roll in and the office of Angel Investigations to officially open. Not that it ever really closed.

After leaving the scene of the fire, Doyle and Angel had gone their separate ways. Angel had headed back to his quarters to consult his reference books, in the hope of turning up some link to fire. Doyle had gone home to shower and stack a few Zs.

Though Angel had to admit he'd had a quick shower, too. The crime scene had stayed with him in a way he hadn't liked. There was something about the smell of seared human flesh that tended to cling and did not appeal.

"You're kidding," Doyle said now as he gazed hopefully around the kitchen. Sometimes, when the team was involved in an all-nighter, Angel cooked breakfast for the human members. Apparently, it hadn't occurred to him to do so today. Probably because he was the only one who'd actually worked all night.

Doyle sidled over to the counter and popped a couple pieces of bread into the toaster. There was nothing wrong with a little initiative, was there?

"Nothing?" he asked.

"It helps if you know what you're looking for," Angel remarked, his tone a little testy. "Do you have any idea how many entities and rituals are associated with fire?"

"Right," Doyle said. "Okay, good point."

Angel slammed shut the book he'd been reading, causing a small mushroom cloud of dust to hover over the table.

"There's got to be a way to narrow the research down."

He got up and prowled around the kitchen, finally coming to rest with his back against the fridge. He could hardly remember the last time he'd felt so useless, so frustrated. So confused. A thing he was pretty sure he hated most of all.

These killings had been going on for months, for *months,* and he'd done nothing about them. But then, in all fairness to himself, neither had the Powers That Be. He had to assume they'd known all along that something big and bad was behind the killings. So why wait until now to clue him in?

"Why don't you take me through the vision again," he suggested to Doyle. "The first thing you saw was the girl, right? The one with red hair?"

"Right," Doyle said again. His toast shot up out of the toaster and into the air. He caught both pieces on the fly, slapped them on a plate. "Excuse me," he said. Obligingly, Angel scooted over, his brow furrowed in concentration.

"Then what?"

"Then there was the streetlight," Doyle answered as he reached past Angel's blood supply to where the butter sat at the back of the fridge. "I saw it explode. Then everything went black. Sort of like a movie fade-out."

Angel's frown got a little deeper. "Has that ever happened before? The fade-out thing?"

Doyle paused. "I don't think so, now that you mention it," he said. "It's usually everything at once, then it's over."

"Interesting."

"Easy for you to say," Doyle said. He began to butter his toast.

"And after the fade-out?" Angel asked.

"After the fade-out came the congregation. Then another fade, then the coin thing, and then the searing-pain-right-between-the-eyes finale," Doyle said. "Though there might have been . . ."

Doyle's voice trailed off as Angel's frown became a full-fledged scowl. Without warning, Angel moved back to the table and began to sort through one of the piles of books.

"You're sure it was a coin?" he asked.

Doyle gave up the attempt to determine whether or not the final image he'd seen, the outline of that human head, had belonged to the vision or to the real world. He hadn't known then. He didn't know now. A thing which was unusual in and of itself. Usually, what was a vision and what wasn't was pretty clear.

"Not a hundred percent sure," he confessed. "I didn't recognize the markings. You think that's the way in?"

"Could be," Angel said. He flipped one book closed, opened another. "I thought there was something . . ."

"You don't have one of those new Sacajawea dollars, do you?" Doyle asked.

"Hmmm?" Angel said, his attention still on the reference books.

"One of the new dollars," Doyle repeated. "I thought the coin thing might be one of them."

Angel slammed the second book closed. This was getting him nowhere fast.

When he'd first come to L.A., Angel had made himself a promise. He would not dwell on those he'd left behind in Sunnydale. It was way too painful, not to mention way too useless. But there were times when thoughts of them came to him anyway.

Like, say, for instance, now.

Having Giles or Willow around would be pretty helpful. Painstaking research had never been Angel's strong point. He'd always been more of an action figure sort of guy.

"You're sure that's all?" he barked at Doyle.

"Pretty sure," Doyle said through a mouthful of toast.

"Well, then we're screwed," Angel announced. "This vision doesn't make any sense. We're supposed to be able to use it to intervene, to save the day, right? So why send us a vision of somebody's death? And why send the vision now? Why not months ago when this whole Krispy Kritter thing began?"

Doyle paused, the piece of toast halfway to his mouth. "Good point," he said. "Unless . . ."

Angel met Doyle's eyes across the table. "Unless," Angel said slowly, "tonight's killing had to happen so we *could* intervene. In which case we're supposed to save somebody we haven't even seen yet."

A beat of silence filled the kitchen.

"Sometimes I really hate this job," Doyle said.

"That makes two of us."

A clatter of feet on the stairs alerted them to Cordelia's arrival. It was time for Angel Investigations to go on the clock for another day. Given what had happened so far, Angel had to wonder what the next twenty-four hours might bring.

Cordy burst into the kitchen, a large white pastry box in her arms. She held it aloft like a trophy.

"Krispy Kreme, anyone?"

CHAPTER FIVE

"I want to talk to you, Lockley," an irate voice said.

Detective Kate Lockley was glad her desk faced at least partway away from the office door. It meant she could permit herself the luxury of rolling her eyes. If there was one thing she didn't need this morning, this was it. A dressing-down from the detective in charge of the Krispy Kritter investigation.

Not that she didn't deserve it.

Kate had been skirting the edges of acceptable protocol for weeks now, and she knew it. She'd had to figure it was only a matter of time before she got her hands slapped. Which wasn't the same as saying she had to be happy about it. Particularly on a morning when she'd just been up half the night before.

Of course, so had the person who wanted to

yell at her, with even more cause. *Sometimes,* Kate thought, *it's a real drag having a sense of fair play.*

She turned toward the door, carefully avoiding the eyes of her co-workers. Equally careful to keep her expression and her voice cool as she answered.

"Something I can do for you, Detective Tucker?"

Detective Jackson Tucker was a relatively new addition to the department, but he'd made his presence felt. Fast. There had been a great deal of speculation about how the new guy had ended up in charge of the Krispy Kritter investigation. Some said it was just that Tucker's number had come up. Others that it stemmed directly from his ability to kiss ass. Though he'd been part of the department for several months now, he'd formed no associations, made no friends. A situation he seemed to like just fine.

He wasn't quite a loner. He worked the system too well for that. But it had always seemed to Kate as if Tucker was surrounded by some sort of invisible force field. His own personal no-fly zone. He never got jostled, glad-handed, slapped on the back. Nobody touched him unless he initiated the contact.

He was different in other ways, too. In a sea of desks overflowing with paperwork, Tucker's work area was always neat as a pin. He was always meticulously dressed in a pair of khaki slacks, button-down shirt, sports jacket. His penny loafers had actual pennies in them.

Kate didn't know where it had come from, but gradually a nickname for Tucker had emerged. Probably in response to all that dedication to perfection. The entire department called him the Hick. Not to his face, of course. His one concession to being human was his legendary temper tantrums.

Of which Kate was about to be a less-than-lucky recipient.

"I want to know what you were doing at my crime scene last night," Tucker said now as he strode purposefully across the room toward her desk. Legs pulled back from aisleways. Arms waving in the air for information or attention were suddenly pulled back over their desks.

It's like the parting of the Red Sea, Kate thought. *Maybe Moses should have been Tucker's nickname.*

"Who says I was there?" she asked.

Detective Tucker leaned across her desk in a deliberate attempt to loom over her. "Don't play games with me, Lockley," he said. "I know you were there. Just like I know you've been asking to see files that are none of your business."

Kate could feel her irritation, like a layer of sand beneath her skin. She knew the smart thing to do would be to back down. Let Tucker win his public pissing contest. That was really all this was about. A little show of manly force, marking territory. All she had to do was to back off and he'd go away.

The trouble was, she just couldn't quite bring herself to do it. Everything about him made her want to hit back, to challenge him. There was probably some deep psychological lesson for her in all this. There was a reason girls didn't have pissing contests, wasn't there?

She flashed the badge pinned to the front of her navy blue blazer. "I'm a cop. Murder *is* my business," she reminded.

Detective Tucker leaned over a little farther, jabbing one finger against her desk blotter. "Not when it's my case, it isn't," he said. "This isn't like you, Lockley," he went on, his tone faintly mocking. "The way I hear it, you're the resident straight-arrow around here. The one who always wants to play by the rules."

As if a new thought had just occurred to him, Tucker stopped looming and stood up straight. He put his hands on his hips, parting his jacket to reveal the gun in its holster strapped underneath.

Subtle, Kate thought. *Like nuclear waste.*

"So what I have to ask myself," Tucker went on, his voice soft and feral, "is just what is little Kate-the-Straight up to?"

Kate was spared the necessity of an answer.

"Hey, Lockley, you got a visitor!" a voice bellowed from the doorway.

One glimpse of the person coming through the door had Kate wincing inwardly. *And the hits just keep on coming,* she thought sarcastically. Her visitor was probably the one person on earth who *could* escalate the current confrontation.

"Hey, Kate. I figured you could use some decent coffee," Deirdre Arensen said.

Kate and Deirdre had been friends since college. Though they hadn't seen all that much of each other, they'd kept in touch in the intervening years. Kate couldn't even really remember the last time she and Deirdre had gotten together, until the other woman had appeared at her desk claiming she might have information that could help the Krispy Kritter investigation.

Kate had had misgivings about Deirdre's story. Plenty of them. But she'd gone ahead and done the right thing. She'd shared the information with Detective Tucker, even going so far as to set up an interview between Tucker and her old friend.

Deirdre had hardly finished her story before Tucker had gone completely ballistic, all but accusing Kate of deliberately attempting to impede his investigation. He'd told Deirdre he never wanted to hear from her again. He'd used words like *Looney Toons* and *nutcase*.

"Well, well, what have we here?" he murmured now, his eyes bright with something that looked an awful lot like pleasure and malice, mixed. "Could it be that the answer to my question just walked in? Is that what you've been doing sniffing around my investigation, Lockley? Feeding information to an old friend?"

Deirdre's progress toward Kate faltered, then slowed to a complete stop as she realized who was standing by Kate's desk. Then Kate saw Deirdre's chin come up and permitted herself an inward grin. Now, *that* was the Deirdre Arensen she knew. Deirdre continued toward Kate's desk, her stride steady and sure.

"Detective," Deirdre said as she set a steaming paper cup down on Kate's blotter.

"Ms. Arensen."

"*Dr.* Arensen," Kate corrected.

Detective Tucker did a bad double-take. "Oh, that's right," he said. "You have a degree, don't you. Parapsychology, wasn't that it?"

"Just plain psychology," Deirdre said. Her eyes were frosty, but they nevertheless met Kate's in a quick and silent apology. "I can come back later, if this is a bad time," she offered.

"No need," Kate said. She stood up behind her desk. It was time for this to be over. Remaining seated with all these people towering over her was beginning to make her feel like a kindergartner. "I think we're all finished here, aren't we, Detective?"

Tucker rounded on her, his expression fierce.

"I'll tell you what's finished, *Detective*," he said. "You will be, if you don't butt out. Mess with my investigation again, and I'll have your badge."

He turned and swaggered out the door, leaving a silent bull pen in his wake. Spontaneously Kate decided there was one more thing she disliked about him. The way he provoked childish reactions in her. She had to resist an impulse to stick her tongue out.

"Whew!" Deirdre exclaimed as she collapsed into the chair beside Kate's desk. "Talk about bad timing. Sorry about that."

"Don't worry about it," Kate said, resuming her own seat and taking a sip of the coffee Deirdre had brought her. "I guess you could say I had some of it coming."

It was unlikely Tucker could really get her fired. It was mostly his ego claiming she was messing with his investigation. But he could definitely make things unpleasant for her with the top brass. And that would embarrass Kate's father, who had recently retired from the force. Kate had learned well and early that her actions reflected on him, too. Fair or not, his retirement didn't change that.

"He wouldn't have come after you if I hadn't asked you to help me," Deirdre insisted.

A statement that was hard for Kate to deny, as it happened to be true.

All of a sudden Kate stood back up. She and

Deirdre needed to discuss the situation, and the place to do it definitely wasn't here. "I could use a break. How about a walk?"

"Sounds good." Deirdre nodded, rising in her turn.

"No kidding," the detective seated at the desk next to Kate's remarked, without looking up. "Anybody else notice there's an awful lot of hot air in here?"

Nobody responded, but, as she walked to the door, Kate was smiling for the first time that day.

"I just don't think there's anything more I can do," she said a few moments later. Kate and Deirdre were seated on a bench at a nearby park. "I'm sorry, Dee. I don't suppose I could talk you into just letting it go? Letting the police do their job?"

Deirdre was silent for a moment. "Is that what you'd do if you were in my place?"

Kate gave a self-deprecating snort. Deirdre had her there, and they both knew it. In fact, she'd pretty much expected her friend to come back with something like this.

"Have I ever mentioned that the fact you've known me so long really sucks sometimes?"

Deirdre's smile was genuine but swift. There and gone in the same instant. "If that pompous, self-important asshole had been willing to listen to me, that girl might still be alive," she said. "You realize that, don't you?"

"Yes," Kate said, though privately she still had her doubts.

This time it was Deirdre who snorted. "You don't fool me, Kate," she said. "You said it yourself. I've known you too long. You don't believe me, either, do you?"

"I don't *not* believe you," Kate replied. "It's just— there's no evidence to support your theory, Dee. Nothing to link any of the other victims to a cult."

"Because I'm the only one willing to look for it," Deirdre answered.

"Maybe," Kate said.

"Look," Deirdre said suddenly. "All this is off the point."

"The point being?" Kate asked.

"The point being that I need to keep going and you can't help me anymore," Deirdre said. She was silent for a moment, sipping her own coffee.

"I don't suppose you know anybody who could help me take this on?" she finally asked. "You know, somebody who walks on the wild side. Tall, dark, and handsome. Slightly mysterious. Not afraid of a close personal relationship with the Dark Side of the Force."

Her tone made it clear she thought it was unlikely there was anyone out there matching her description.

"Funny you should ask," Kate said. "As a matter of fact, I just might."

CHAPTER SIX

"You're still up for this, right?" Andy asked.

Terri rubbed suddenly sweaty palms down the front of her best skirt, hoping he didn't notice the nervous gesture.

"Of course I am," she said.

She'd been telling herself that ever since yesterday, all through her sleepless night and the long day that had followed. *It's a good thing I had the day off today,* she thought. She'd been so pre-occupied she'd probably have done something stupid like try to make up the beds with towels instead of sheets at the motel where she worked.

The chance of a lifetime. That's what Andy'd called it.

And now he was asking if she was up for it. Up for throwing off her cloak of invisibility and being somebody at last. Was she ready? Oh, yes, she certainly thought so.

But being certain didn't make her any less nervous. If anything, Terri thought, it made her more. She'd tried her best to block it out, but all night long, all through the day, her mother's voice had lectured from the back of Terri's mind.

"Don't wish for things too much, Terri Nicole. You'll wind up disappointed, just like always."

Shut up, Mama, Terri thought now. *I don't want to listen. I won't listen. Because you aren't going to be right this time.*

She pinched the pad of her left hand, then winced. Since meeting Andy in the parking lot last night, she'd performed that action about a million times. Making sure she was awake. That she hadn't dreamed up the whole encounter.

She sneaked a look at Andy, confidently piloting the car. No, this wasn't a dream. And even if it was, Terri definitely preferred it to real life. She folded her hands in her lap to keep them still. If this was a delusion, she didn't want to know. If a dream, she'd rather not wake up.

They were riding in Andy's car tonight. A street-hugging black Corvette. Terri had almost passed out when she'd seen it pulling up in front of her apartment. Every time she heard the engine growl as Andy shifted gears, Terri's heart gave a kick of excitement. Just riding in the car made her feel like a whole new person. Her mother would have an absolute fit if she could see her now.

"Let me tell you about guys who drive cars like that. They're only after one thing, you know."

That's what Mama would have said. Then she'd give that little sniff that always signaled she was about to say something she considered terribly clever. Usually a thing to make Terri feel even worse than normal.

"Not that you'll ever have to worry about that, Terri Nicole."

Right, Mom. Like you ever did. Terri bit back an unexpected smile. She kind of liked the way she was answering back, even if it was only inside her head. Before meeting Andy, she'd never even done that before.

Andy took a turn, and the car began to climb. "You're awfully quiet," he observed. "Having second thoughts?"

"No," Terri denied swiftly. Not exactly. She'd had so many different ones over the last twenty-four hours, she'd passed the second-thoughts stage a long time ago.

"You meant it, didn't you?" she suddenly burst out. "Everything you said last night. I mean, you didn't just feel sorry for me and—"

"Come on now, Terri," Andy interrupted. "We've been through this before. That's why I wanted you to come with me tonight. Because I *do* know how you feel. That whole thing about being invisible."

"But not for the same reason," Terri countered.

Andy took another turn. "No," he acknowledged. "But I thought I explained. Good looks can be a curse, too, you know. All anybody's ever interested in is your face, particularly in a place like L.A. They don't care who you are—*that* you are—inside."

"But you changed all that," Terri said. "When you joined the Illuminati."

That was the name of the group he was taking her to meet. He'd told her it meant the Enlightened Ones.

"I didn't change other people," Andy said. "I changed myself. My own perspective. That's one of the first things you learn to do as an Illuminati."

He glanced over at her, swiftly, then back at the road. "Think about it, Terri," he went on. "Why worry about what other people think? *You're* the one who's important. I'm hoping the meeting tonight will help you see that."

Terri felt some of her nervousness begin to ease. This was just what he'd said last night. "You mean you're hoping I see the light?" she quipped.

Andy smiled and took one hand off the wheel to give hers a quick squeeze. "That's more like it," he said. "Not much farther now."

For the first time Terri noticed her surroundings. "Hey," she said. "Where are we?"

"Over toward the coast," Andy said. "Did I mention every meeting happens in a different location? Part of that whole change of perspective thing I was talking about. This one should be pretty cool. It's in this exclusive hotel right above the beach."

Terri felt her nervousness return with a vengeance, a hard lump in her stomach.

"Will there be important people there?" she asked.

Andy shot her a sideways look of reproof. "We're all important people," he said. "Do I have to say, 'Repeat after me'?"

Terri attempted a laugh. "I'll get back to you on that one."

Without warning, Andy slowed. He took a sharp turn to the right, gearing down as the car growled up a steep, narrow drive lined with tall hedges. At the crest of the hill he braked before a pair of wrought-iron gates. On either side Terri could see security cameras.

"Last chance to turn back," Andy said.

"No," Terri said quickly. "No, I'm okay. I want to go on."

In a gesture that had Terri's breath backing up in her lungs, Andy reached over and ran one finger lightly down her cheek.

"I can't tell you how happy I am to hear you say that."

The meeting of the Illuminati was like nothing Terri had imagined.

In the first place, there was the hotel itself. She still didn't know its name. There had been nothing to identify it as Andy had ushered her into its plush lobby. As they'd come through the doors, Terri had caught her breath. The entire lower level seemed comprised of windows overlooking the ocean. It made Terri feel as if she were walking on a cloud, hovering in midair.

"Talk about change in perspective," she'd murmured.

Andy had flashed her a grin. "You ain't seen nothin' yet."

While he was speaking, an attractive young woman wearing basic black and pearls came out from behind the front desk.

"A pleasure to have you with us this evening," she said. "If you'll step this way—" She gestured across the lobby and down a corridor to the right.

Terri was half afraid she'd trip and fall as she followed Andy and the hotel staff member across the lobby. The carpet was so thick it came all the way up to her instep. The young woman paused at the entrance to the hallway.

"Last door to the left," she said. "Please don't hesitate to let us know if there's any additional way in which we may be of service." Then she pivoted neatly on one foot and moved gracefully back toward the desk.

Andy took Terri by the elbow and piloted her down the hall.

"Showtime," he said.

Like the rest of the hotel Terri had seen so far, the room in which the Illuminati would hold their meeting also had big windows overlooking the ocean. In front of them several small semicircles of chairs faced a discreet podium.

Though Terri's first impression was that the room was full, she soon realized it was because the Illuminati didn't sit beside one another. Each member had his or her own seat, with empty seats on either side. Each one faced straight ahead, as if waiting for the meeting to start. No one was doing any socializing. No catching up on how things had gone since the last time they'd gotten together. It was as if they had nothing in common at all.

"This okay?" Andy asked as he guided Terri to a seat in the mostly empty back row.

"Sure," Terri said. She moved a few seats into the row and sat down. The only other occupant was a young man in a well-tailored business suit sitting at the far end. Terri expected Andy to join her, but he lingered in the aisle.

"I have to go take care of some things up front," he said. "Now, don't worry about anything, all right? You're going to be just fine. I'll see you after the meeting's over."

Without waiting for an answer, Andy moved off. Terri felt all her nervousness return. *Don't just leave me!* she thought. Something of what she was feeling must have shown in her face. The young man at the other end of the row looked over at her and gave her an encouraging smile.

Andy's version of taking care of some things up front turned out to be running the meeting. Terri felt a moment of panic shoot through her as he stepped up in front of the podium to call the meeting to order. Surely only a group leader did things like that. Why hadn't Andy told her he was so important?

It must have been to spare my feelings, Terri thought. *He knew how nervous I was.* At the front of the room Andy had begun to introduce the first speaker.

He probably realized I might not have come with him if he'd told me he was the group leader right off, Terri's inner monologue went on. She'd have been too intimidated. The information that he was someone important would only have made her feel even more like the nobody she was.

But she was going to stop thinking like that, she told herself firmly as Andy stepped aside to make room for a woman in designer workout togs. Everybody in this room was important, including Terri herself. Hadn't Andy just said so?

Twenty minutes later Terri had forgotten every qualm she'd ever had. All she wanted was to sign on the dotted line.

So far, there'd been four speakers. The four newest members. Although the details were different, they'd all told essentially the same story. They'd been unhappy, unfulfilled. Before. Now they were living the lives they were meant to live, the ones they'd always dreamed of. And they owed it all to just one thing: Becoming an Enlightened One. Joining the Illuminati.

Terri joined in the applause as the current speaker, a man who'd saved his family's orange groves and now had a thriving microbusiness providing local organically grown orange juice to restaurants in Beverly Hills, finished his testimonial and sat down. As Andy moved back to the podium, Terri felt unexpected movement at her side.

Automatically she shifted position, making room for the latecomer. Out of the corner of her eye, she could see it was a woman, a striking blonde. Hair the color of Kansas cornsilk. Skin, porcelain-fine. With a shock, Terri realized she knew who this was: rising daytime-TV star Joy Clement. Pronounced in the French way. Cluh-mahn.

Just last week she'd swept aside the actress who'd previously been considered a shoo-in to win an award for her portrayal of the innocent-looking schemer Natalie Bishop on the daytime drama *Yesterday, Today, Tomorrow*. Rumors of a soon-to-be-made feature film filled the trade magazines.

As if sensing Terri's scrutiny, Joy's head turned in Terri's direction. Terri could feel herself being swiftly appraised, even though a pair of dark glasses obscured the other woman's eyes.

"You're new, aren't you?" Joy whispered, leaning a little closer. "You haven't joined?"

Terri shook her head. "But I'm going to," she whispered back. "Just as soon as I—"

"And now it gives me great pleasure to introduce our final speaker," Andy said from the podium. "I'm sure you don't need me to tell you how proud we are of her. She's one of our greatest success stories."

He held a hand out in a welcoming gesture to the back of the room. "Please join me in extending a warm welcome to Miss Joy Clement."

Beside her, Terri felt Joy pull in a deep breath, as if gathering courage. *Maybe she still gets stage fright,* Terri thought. Some of the most famous actors in the world did that, she'd read. Then, to Terri's complete astonishment, Joy rested a hand on her shoulder as she rose to her feet.

"Promise me you'll listen to what I have to say," she murmured, her voice low and intense. For Terri's ears alone. *"Promise."*

Terri stared upward, afraid that she was gaping and it showed. She literally didn't know what else to do.

"I promise," she vowed.

In the next moment Joy Clement was completely transformed. She lifted her hand from Terri's shoulder and waved to the small group of assembled Illuminati as if they were a teeming premiere screening crowd. As she stepped into the aisle and made her way to the podium, she was smiling confidently.

Joy reached the podium, gracefully tilting her face up so that Andy could kiss her on both cheeks. The applause picked up a notch. Then Andy stepped aside, and Joy moved to stand behind the podium. The applause continued, even after she was in position. She stood absolutely still for several seconds, then raised a hand.

"Thank you," she said. "Thank you so much." The applause died down. "Like the others who've spoken tonight, I'm here to testify to the great debt I owe to the Illuminati. To acknowledge the fact that, like you, becoming a member of this organization has proved to be the great turning point in my life."

Her words brought on another brief smattering of applause.

"But as I stand here before you, I wonder—" Joy's voice faltered, then broke off. With a hand that even Terri, seated at the back of the room, could see was trembling, she reached up and pulled away her sunglasses, revealing ravaged, red-rimmed eyes. She looked as if she'd been crying for days without stopping. The image of a self-confident star was completely destroyed.

"I can't help but wonder what kind of price we're going to pay for our successes. I can't help but wonder what in God's name we've truly done."

Terri could have sworn she heard the audience catch its collective breath before the room was filled with absolute silence. She caught a flash of movement out of the corner of her eye. From both sides of the room, men she hadn't noticed before were converging on the podium, moving swiftly and purposefully up the side aisles.

"Think about it," Joy said now, her voice rising in fear and urgency. "Think about what it is we've truly done. Your new life came with a price tag attached, didn't it? *Didn't it?*"

The men reached the podium. They gripped Joy by both arms. She began to struggle, bucking and twisting.

"Don't you see?" she shouted. "The price is too high! We've sold our very souls!"

What's going on? Terri wondered. What was Joy talking about? Had the pressure of success suddenly become too much for her? Were they all the horrified witnesses to a nervous breakdown?

Do something, Andy, Terri thought. Almost as if he'd heard her silent prayer, he stepped forward.

"All right now, Joy, calm down. That's enough."

Joy Clement stopped struggling. Tears began to stream down her face. "Too high," she said again. "The price is too high, Andy. I'm sorry, but I can't pay it after all."

"All right," Andy said again. "I'll take care of it, Joy."

At his words all the color faded from Joy Clement's face. The last impulse to fight seemed to go right out of her. Andy made a gesture. The men on either side of Joy released her. She collapsed forward into Andy's arms.

"Ladies and gentlemen, if you'll just give me a moment—" Andy said. There was a smattering of applause as Andy began to lead Joy toward the exit door. She went docilely, without protesting, until they reached Terri's row. Then, without warning, Joy's head whipped up.

"You promised," she said in a tortured voice.

Terri felt a chill shoot through her as Joy's eyes locked on hers. Terri had been so sure she knew what it felt like to have hit rock bottom, to have nothing left to lose. So sure, until now. But nothing she'd ever experienced had prepared her for what she saw in Joy Clement's eyes.

She looked like a woman who knew her life was over. Who knew, beyond a shadow of a doubt, that she had absolutely nothing left to live for.

"You promised," Joy said once more. "You know you did. It's not too late. Don't join! Save yourself."

"Joy," Andy said, his voice a warning.

The sound of it seemed to snap the last thread of Joy's self-control.

"Don't do it!" she shouted at Terri, twisting in Andy's arms. "Don't join. You don't know them— don't know what they really are. It's not too late. *It's not too late.* You can do it! You can save yourself!"

She was still screaming as Andy pulled her from the room. The sound of her voice cut off abruptly as the door slammed closed.

Terri sat perfectly still, eyes on her hands clasped tightly in her lap. She was certain she could feel the eyes of other people in the room upon her. *Don't look up,* she told herself over and over. She wasn't sure what had just happened, but she was sure of one thing. She'd make up her own mind about whether or not to become a member of the Illuminati. She didn't know Joy Clement, didn't owe her anything. And she was not about to let the other woman's ravings spoil things for her.

"Whew!" a low voice from nearby said. "Pretty heavy, huh?"

Cautiously Terri glanced over at the speaker, the dark-haired young man at the far end of her row. His face wore the same expression Terri figured hers did. Nervous confusion.

It's all right. He's new, just like I am, she thought.

"Definitely heavy," she whispered back.

The guy glanced around, then scooted a couple of chairs closer. "So," he said. "What do you think her story was?"

Terri looked around, too, concerned that they'd attracted attention. They hadn't. The Illuminati were still stonily facing straight forward.

"I don't know," Terri answered honestly. "She asked me if I'd joined yet, and when I said no, she made me promise to listen to what she had to say."

The guy beside her made a face. "As if there was any way to avoid it."

"Yeah," Terri agreed. "Though I don't know what she was talking about. I figure maybe the stress of fame got to be too much for her." She ventured her theory. "Maybe she had some sort of breakdown?"

The guy nodded, as if agreeing with her assessment. Behind her, Terri heard the door click open. Andy came back into the room. He didn't glance in her direction but strode at once toward the podium. All of a sudden, Terri realized how tense and still the room truly was.

Make things all right, Andy, she found herself praying silently. She didn't want this to turn out to be an impossible dream. She wanted a new life, just like the Illuminati offered.

Andy stepped behind the podium, reaching around it with his arms to grasp it on both sides. As if, by his gesture, he was reaching out to embrace the audience as well.

"My friends," he said. "I—" He paused for a moment, as if uncertain how to go on. "My friends, I apologize."

Terri felt a breath of relief move through the room.

"I'm sure I don't need to tell you I had a very special goal in mind when I asked Joy Clement to come and speak to us tonight. To offer hope. To inspire. On the surface, I've failed in that goal. But if you look deeper, *if you change your perspective,* I think you'll see the silver lining to this evening's dark cloud.

"Joy's unfortunate behavior has reminded us of one thing we can never afford to let ourselves forget: Becoming one of us is not for everyone."

"Hear, hear!" a voice in the front row cried. Terri felt the rest of the tension in the room dissolve abruptly. She leaned forward, determined to drink in Andy's every word.

This, she was sure, was the heart of what she had come for.

"We are special," Andy continued. "Unique. Select. *Enlightened.* Not chosen, for we recognize that we are the ones who choose. To be true to ourselves, to live our own lives as authentically as possible."

For the first time the Illuminati seemed to come to life. Terri saw heads in front of her begin to nod.

"But Joy was right about one thing, wasn't she?"

Andy asked. The murmur ceased. The room grew silent. "The price of enlightenment is high."

I don't care. I don't care, Terri thought wildly. *Whatever the price is, I'm willing to pay it.*

"Becoming an Illuminati means you must give up something, doesn't it?" Andy went on. "You all had to do it. You know what I mean. I'm talking about the past, aren't I?

"Choosing to become Enlightened means just that. It means you choose the light. And where does the light shine most brightly? In the present. Not in the past. Not even in the future. But in the time and place in which we truly lead our lives. The here. The *now.*"

Terri could feel her heart begin to pound in hard, fast strokes against her ribs. She felt lightheaded. Spots danced before her eyes. She was so excited, she feared for a moment that she'd be sick.

Here it was, at last. The chance she'd wished her whole life for. To be free of the pain and humiliation others had heaped upon her. To do more than forget the past. More even than render it unimportant. To wipe it out, as if it had never existed at all. Then to create herself all over again. This time in the image that *she* wanted.

She kept her eyes glued to Andy as he stepped out from behind the podium and began to move slowly, yet steadily down the aisle.

"Joy wasn't the only person I asked to come

here tonight," he said. "I also brought a new-comer. Terri, will you please stand up?"

Leg muscles quivering as if she'd just run a race, Terri slowly rose to her feet.

"Everybody, this is Terri."

"Hi, Terri," murmured the assembled Illuminati.

Andy stopped at the end of Terri's row.

"You know what time it is now, don't you? It's time for you to make a decision. Do you want to join us, or not? If you choose not to join, I want you to know there'll be no hard feelings. But if your answer is no, I'll have to ask you to step out-side. The rest of the meeting is business for true Illuminati only. There can be no outsiders."

At the word *outsider* Terri felt something in her head explode. That's what she'd been, that's *all* she'd been, her whole life. But no more.

After tonight nobody would ever suggest that she wasn't important again. Try to tell her that she didn't belong. From now on, things were going to be different. She was going to make them different. She was going to *be* someone.

Andy held out a hand, as if in invitation.

"Well, Terri," he said. "Do you have an answer for me? Will you join us and become an Enlight-ened One?"

Terri felt herself moving forward as confidently as a model down a runway.

"I will," she said as fervently as if she were speaking a marriage vow.

"Me, too. I want to join, too!" a nearby voice cried. Terri turned to see the guy who'd been in the row beside her rushing down the aisle. She held her hand out, as if welcoming him into the chain of enlightenment.

Around her, the assembled Illuminati burst into spontaneous applause.

He loved fire. Even those he marked had no idea how much. Had no idea that, when he set up the chain of events that would consign them to the flames, he didn't think of it as punishment, as inflicting pain. Rather, he was giving them the privilege of being consumed by, becoming a servant to, the thing he loved the most.

He wasn't sure he could explain it, his fascination. His devotion. It seemed he'd always had it. So he'd long since given up any attempt to try. He only knew his love had made him perfect what he had to do. A thing not even the police had guessed.

He was going to set the whole world on fire.

He smiled now, humming as he moved about the kitchen late at night. Turning the gas burner on the stove up to High to warm some soup.

And the tune he hummed was "You Light Up My Life."

CHAPTER SEVEN

"So, tell me who this guy is again?" Deirdre Arensen asked as she and Kate got out of the car. "You're being kind of mysterious about him. That's not like you."

Kate shrugged as they started toward the building that housed Angel Investigations. "He's just this P.I. I know."

It had taken her a couple of days to actually carry through on her promise to put Deirdre in touch with someone who might be able to help her continue her own investigation into the Krispy Kritter killings. It wasn't that she didn't want to help . . .

Okay, be honest, Lockley, Kate told herself. It probably was.

The truth was, Kate had always had misgivings about her friend's decision to pursue the Krispy Kritter on her own. And it wasn't just that she was talking about going after one of the most vicious, to say nothing of efficient, killers the City of Angels had ever known.

It was also because of the fact that Deirdre wanted to investigate for personal reasons. Not that Kate couldn't sympathize. But, as a cop, she'd been taught—and she genuinely believed—that being emotionally involved in a case was a hindrance, not a selling point.

Being in too close made it hard to see things clearly. And if one didn't see clearly, one made mistakes. Sometimes fatal ones. Enough lives had been lost already. Kate didn't want Deirdre to lose hers, also.

The thing that had finally convinced Kate to follow through and actually call Angel had been the same thing that had prompted her to try to help Deirdre herself. She knew Deirdre Arensen. Knew that she would never back down. She'd pursue the Krispy Kritter Killer to the ends of the earth. If she had to, she'd do it on her own.

The way Kate had it figured, that made Deirdre more of a danger to herself than to anybody else. Kate also had to figure it left *her* out of options. Deirdre was smart, but she wasn't a trained investigator. Kate was, but she couldn't be directly involved anymore. If she wanted to protect her friend, she had to have backup. Even if it wasn't the kind she usually called for.

Kate opened the door to the office building.

"So, you going to tell me how you met him?" Deirdre asked as the two women made their way across the slightly dusty lobby. "Or do I have to get tough and bring out the rubber hose?"

"Oh, wow. That's got me scared," Kate said. It ought to be simple, explaining about Angel. But somehow, it never was. Probably, Kate thought, because there was nothing simple about *him*. And because there was still so much about him that she didn't know.

"I met him working a case," she finally said. "How else?"

Deirdre gave a quick laugh. "Don't tell me, you thought he was a suspect, right?"

Kate gave her a startled glance. "Actually, I did," she acknowledged. "How did you know?"

Deirdre Arensen shook her head, as if she couldn't believe Kate had actually asked the question. "You forget how well I know you. Much as I hate to admit it, that prick of a detective is right about one thing, Kate. You've always been a straight arrow."

Kate was surprised to feel her face coloring. What was so bad about having high ideals? A belief that there was a real and tangible difference between what was right and what was wrong? It wasn't that she didn't believe there were shades of gray. She just didn't believe there were nearly as many of them as other people thought.

"Yeah?" she said. "So?"

Deirdre gave her quick laugh again and laid a hand on Kate's arm. "Now don't go getting all hurt feelings on me," she said. "I just meant it stands to reason, that's all.

"You say you'll help me, take days to follow through, then when you finally do agree to take me to meet this guy you won't tell me anything about him. I have to figure he pushes your buttons, somehow. So when you tell me you met him working on a case, the obvious assumption is that you pegged him for a suspect."

"Jeez," Kate said. "With deductive skills like that you should have been a lawyer."

"Well, there's no need to insult me," Deirdre answered as they proceeded down the hall. "Just tell me this. Do you trust him?"

As they approached it, the door marked Angel Investigations swung open, and a man with dark hair stuck his head out.

"Ah, Detective Lockley and damsel in distress. Come right this way. We've been waitin' for ya."

Deirdre shot Kate a look. "Great. Fantastic," she murmured under her breath as the two women stepped into the office. "I ask for help and you set me up with someone who sounds like he stepped out of *Darby O'Gill and the Little People.*"

"That's not Angel," Kate whispered back. "And the answer to your question is yes, I do trust him."

❧   ❧   ❧

Deirdre Arensen reminded Angel of a vixen. In the *National Geographic* sense of the term. A female fox, rather than a provocative, foxy female. Though he had to admit it was likely she was those things, too.

The coloring wasn't right, of course. Deirdre's hair was dark brown, not a fox's astonishing burnished auburn. But she had the broad forehead, wide-spaced eyes, and pointed chin that always reminded Angel of the animals he'd sometimes hunted in his youth.

Foxes were smart and indefatigable. They also had sharp teeth they weren't afraid to use. He wondered how many of these qualities Deirdre possessed. From his brief conversation on the phone with Kate, he had to figure on at least the first two.

"Have a seat," he said as Doyle ushered Kate and Deirdre into what passed as the Angel Investigations conference room. It was actually Angel's hastily tidied-up office.

"I'm Angel," he said. "This is Doyle."

Deirdre glanced back over her shoulder as she and Kate sat down.

"Something I can get you?" Angel inquired.

"No," she said, turning back around. "I just wondered if you were hiding Madonna and Cher around here somewhere."

So much for the question of sharp teeth, Angel thought. "I thought we'd just start out on a first-name basis," he said.

"Actually, Doyle's my last name," Doyle reminded.

"What's your first name?" Deirdre asked.

Doyle shook his head. "Not in this lifetime."

"At least that has more syllables than Doyle." Without warning, Deirdre Arensen grinned, the expression lighting up her entire face. Making her dark eyes sparkle. Then, as swiftly as it had come, the smile was gone. She turned to Kate, her expression deadly serious.

"Okay," she said. "Let's get this show on the road."

In response, Kate reached into a large shoulder bag and removed a copy of a police crime-scene photo.

"They let you take those when it's not your case?" Angel asked.

Kate's eyes met his calmly. "No."

She slapped the photo in the very center of the table, facing Angel, and he forgot all about the etiquette of police inquiries. Even to his eyes, and they'd seen a lot, the image in the photograph was nothing less than horrible.

Fire did strange things to the human anatomy, things most people didn't know, or didn't care to think about. It boiled brains, exploded them out of the backs of skulls. Melted skin, fused sinew to bone. The body in the picture was curled in upon itself like some grotesque imitation of a sleeping child. A child with its fists up, ready to fight.

There was a Post-It note attached to the bottom of the photo. On it was written "Martin Arensen" and a date of just a few weeks ago.

Angel's eyes shot up to Deirdre's. He found them hot and dry. Filled not with sorrow but with a fierce determination.

She jabbed a finger against the photograph, her eyes never leaving Angel's.

"I want you to help me nail the son of a bitch who did this to my father."

"My father came to L.A. a couple of months ago," Deirdre went on. "Actually, he kept a sort of home base here, in Malibu, though he hardly ever used it. He traveled too much, because of his job."

"Which was?"

Deirdre took a sip of the coffee Doyle had recently gotten up to provide, grimaced as the thick, bitter liquid seared her tastebuds, and quickly set the cup back down. Her revelation that her father was one of the Krispy Kritter victims had explained part of the reason for her visit, though not all.

Kate had said Deirdre had a theory, one the police didn't put much stock in. One Kate hadn't wanted to discuss over the phone. She'd let Deirdre do that in person, she'd said. All she asked was that Angel keep an open mind.

Under different circumstances the request might have amused him. Kate Lockley had no idea just how open Angel's mind could be. A status quo that actually suited him just fine.

"Dad was a cult deprogrammer," Deirdre said. "One of the best."

"You mean one of those guys who kidnaps people and—"

"*Doyle.*"

Doyle's head jerked in Angel's direction. "Right, okay. I can see I phrased that badly," he said. He switched his attention back to Deirdre. "What I *meant* to say was that your dad was one of those guys who helped misguided youth see the error of their ways. And he wasn't afraid to use a little tough love."

Deirdre Arensen gave him a faint smile. "Actually, that's not a bad description," she acknowledged. "The profession has something of a bad rap, but Dad genuinely believed in what he was doing. He hated anything that he thought smacked of coercion or brainwashing."

"People are not just sheep on two legs," Kate suddenly spoke up.

Deirdre nodded. "I heard that one often enough."

"Did you follow in his footsteps?" Angel asked.

Deirdre shook her head. "Not really, though I do have a degree in psychology. Unlike my father, I don't work with people much. I'm more of an academic. Dad always said I got sucked in by the lure of the ivory tower.

"I guess you could say my area of expertise is the psychology of folklore. I'm interested in the way certain kinds of themes recur in myth and folklore from culture to culture, even when those societies are geographically isolated. And, naturally, whether or not those themes stem from the same psychological causes."

Interesting, Angel thought. He wouldn't have pegged the determined woman seated across from him as an academic. But then, his first impressions of people had been known to be wrong.

Still, there was something about Deirdre Arensen. *Undercurrents,* Angel thought. He had a feeling the self-possessed surface she presented to the world was only one part of her. It was the parts he hadn't been allowed to see yet that would tell him who she really was. Assuming he ever found out at all.

He nodded, to show he was following her explanation. "Okay, I get the idea. Go on."

"A lot of what I do is pretty straightforward," Deirdre continued. "Everybody has a cycle of creation myths, that sort of stuff. But what interests me is what I guess you'd call the more far-out elements."

Deirdre's lips twisted in a self-deprecating smile.

"At least, that's what my professors always thought. My specialty is the way various cultures depict the supernatural. The way they try to put a name and face to the things they can't explain. That scare them. You know, the things that go bump in the night."

"Sounds fascinating," Angel commented.

Doyle gave a sudden cough.

"I used to think so," Deirdre said. Abruptly her lecture-hall demeanor seemed to desert her. She tapped her fingers against the rim of her coffee cup in an agitated, restless gesture Angel was pretty sure she didn't even notice.

"The thing you have to understand is that I never *believed* in any of it. It was just an intellectual exercise. Find the common themes. Compare and contrast. Then I—"

She paused and pulled in a deep breath.

"I found something. Something I thought would interest my father. I never would have told him, if I'd thought for a moment—"

"Found what?" Angel prompted.

Deirdre eyed him from across the table. Plainly, now that the moment of truth had come, she was experiencing a moment of reluctance. She glanced at Kate, who raised her eyebrows at her. Deirdre murmured something Angel couldn't quite catch under her breath and Kate smiled.

"This is where the police checked out," Deirdre said, her voice a challenge. "Where they told me I was emotionally distraught over the death of my father and ought to have my head examined."

"I'm not the police," Angel said.

Deirdre gave a harsh laugh. "God, I hope not."

Again, she paused. Angel waited. A thing he was good at. One tended to develop certain skills when one was more than two hundred years old.

"Oh, what the hell," Deirdre finally said. "I suppose the first time somebody calls you a nutcase is always the worst, right? And it is why I came here after all.

"I found evidence of a cult. A fire-demon cult."

"Oh, no. Those guys are the worst," said Doyle.

CHAPTER EIGHT

"I don't know how long ago it started," Deirdre continued without so much as a glance in Doyle's direction. Plainly, she thought he was having her on.

"I've been searching, but I can't seem to find the origins. All I've been able to find is the pattern, one I've never seen before. That's one of the reasons I thought it would interest my father. There are lots of references to cults or secret societies dying out, but I'd never seen one that died out and then later somehow managed to resurrect itself."

"Sounds like a recurring nightmare," Kate commented.

Deirdre gave her short, harsh laugh once more. "You got that in one. I told my dad what I thought I'd found, then I—" She pulled in a deep breath, as if steeling herself to continue. "I pretty much set it aside. It was interesting, sure, but cults just aren't what I focus on. I figured I'd passed on an interesting historical anomaly, nothing more. Then I got a phone call from him."

"When was this?" Angel interrupted.

Deirdre's brow furrowed in concentration. "I'd say about a month ago. He said he thought he'd found evidence that the cult had resurfaced in Los Angeles. I've never heard him sound so excited. He even claimed he'd found a cult member who wanted out and was willing to talk. It was so incredible, I didn't believe him at first. Maybe if I had—"

Her voice faltered, then broke off. She cleared her throat with a ruthless sound. "If I had, I could have warned him in time."

"You've got to stop thinking like that, Dee," Kate put in quietly. "It doesn't help, and it will only cloud your judgment."

Deirdre gave her an unamused smile. "My old friend Detective Lockley is big on telling me I need to focus on the facts," she told Angel in a hard, tight voice. "And the *fact* is that, after my dad called, I dug a little deeper and realized there was more to this cult that I'd originally thought.

"As far as I can tell, it's completely deadly. No one attempting to leave it or expose it has ever survived. The records talk about a way the cult identifies those it targets for death. A mark of some kind. When I tried to contact my father to tell him he might be in danger, I couldn't get through. The next day I got the call."

"You think your father's death is tied in to the fire-demon cult," Angel stated.

Deirdre Arensen nodded. "I do, absolutely. He's investigating a fire cult. He dies by fire. That's too much coincidence for me. Unfortunately, the police didn't agree. They see it as a classic serial-killer case. The means of death is just a little more visible than usual.

"According to the detective in charge of the investigation, my father is the only victim whose death might point to the existence of a cult. And the minute I said the words *fire demon*, he totally checked out. Told me if I showed up with my harebrained theory again, he'd have me carted off to a psych ward."

"Nice," Angel said. He glanced at Kate. "Anyone I know?"

Kate shook her head. "Not if you're lucky."

"So what is it you want me to do?" Angel asked Deirdre.

She leaned forward, her expression intent. "I want you to help me find them. Find the cult, if there is one. Uncover what's really going on. But I have to tell you I can't guarantee your safety. This could be dangerous in ways I can't even begin to predict. I want you to know that, right up front."

"No problem."

Deirdre gave a quick laugh and sat back, her expression obviously surprised. "Just like that?"

"Not quite," Angel replied. "If I take this on, there would have to be some ground rules."

Ones he had a feeling were not going to go over big.

"Such as?"

He decided it would be better not to mince words. Deirdre Arensen was a straight shooter if ever he saw one.

"Such as you're no longer directly involved. You came to me—that means you should let my team handle things from here on out."

Deirdre's expression became faintly derisive. "Your team being you and Doyle."

Abruptly Angel stood up. He ran the risk of offending Kate, but the truth was he did not have time for this kind of power-play stuff. To begin with, he wasn't good at it, not to mention the fact that things were already bad enough. Nearly a dozen people dead, and the Powers That Be had just let it happen.

Besides, he'd finally gotten somewhere with all his research. Aside from the fact that her father had been an early Krispy Kritter victim, Deirdre Arensen wasn't telling Angel anything he didn't already know. Better to take her out of the picture and get on with things. She'd be safer that way. He didn't want her added to the body count.

"I think we can call this meeting over, Ms. Arensen," he said. "I'm sorry about your father. Thank you for your time."

"Hey, wait! You can't do that," Deirdre protested.

"It's my office. I can do whatever I want."

"I thought you said you were prepared to help me."

"Not if it involves you dismissing my team right from the start. There's a certain relationship that needs to exist between investigator and client. Maybe you've heard of it. Step one is called trust. If you're not prepared to trust my judgment, you're in the wrong room."

Deirdre glanced at Kate, as if expecting intervention. Kate remained silent.

"Okay, all right, I'm sorry," Deirdre said. She ran a hand through her hair in a gesture of frustration. "Look, will you please just sit back down?"

Angel sat. He took his time.

"And I apologize to Mr. Doyle," Deirdre went on. "I shouldn't have made a snap judgment. I'm sure there's more to you than meets the eye."

Doyle smiled at her, seemingly unoffended. "Regular Columbo, that's me."

Deirdre exhaled a shaky laugh. "Okay," she said. "You guys have made your point." She switched her attention back to Angel. "But you can't ask me to give this up now. I've come too far. I started it, and I—"

"You didn't start anything," Angel countered.

"Don't play word games with me," Deirdre said hotly. "That isn't what I meant and you know it. My father never would have gotten involved with these people if it hadn't been for me. He's dead, and the *fact* is that if I led him to them, then I'm responsible."

Angel opened his mouth to speak, but Deirdre rode right over him.

"Let me tell you something," she said. "Something not even Kate knows. I swore a vow on my father's grave that I would see justice done. You can help me find out who did this—or not. Your choice. But you won't stop me. If I have to, I'll do this on my own."

"She will, you know," Kate spoke up suddenly. "You'll never get her to give up. You won't even get her to back off. She's always been this way. Like a bloodhound."

"Last time it was a pit bull," Deirdre said with a small smile.

"Whatever," Kate answered easily.

"But I notice either way it's still a dog."

"Think of it this way," Kate told Angel. "If she's working with you, at least you can keep an eye on her."

"You keep an eye on her," Angel said.

"I tried."

ANGEL

"I hate it when people talk about me as if I'm not here," Deirdre put in.

"I know what you mean," Doyle commiserated cheerfully. "Happens to me all the time."

"Okay, look," Angel said. "Maybe we can compromise."

After all, Kate did have a point. A loose cannon was the last thing any of them needed. Deirdre working with Angel in some capacity was a lot better than Deirdre on her own. And there was always the chance that Doyle would have another vision. One showing that Deirdre Arensen was the one they were supposed to help.

"You can help do research, maybe even some supervised fieldwork. But where the safety of the team is concerned, we agree right now that I'm the one in charge. We get into a dicey situation, and you do what I say when I say it. No arguments."

Deirdre made a face. "Don't you think that's just a little macho?"

"Take it or leave it," Angel said.

"I'll take it. How soon do we start?"

"I'll want to see—" Angel began.

He was interrupted by the sound of Kate's beeper going off. She checked it quickly, pushed back her chair.

"Sorry," she said. "My time's up. I'll have to go." She glanced at Deirdre. "You can get back to the apartment okay?"

"Well, gee, I think so," Deirdre answered. "I've

been able to drive on my own for quite some time now."

Kate made an exasperated sound. "One more thing," she said to Angel. "This information hasn't been released yet, pending notification of next of kin, but the fire's last victim has been identified as a woman named Ellen Bradshaw."

Deirdre's head jerked around.

"Okay," Angel said. "Any particular reason that's important?"

"According to my father's files," Deirdre filled in, "he hoped Ellen Bradshaw was going to be his cult informant. I got in touch with her after his death. She was absolutely terrified. Claimed the cult had found out what she'd been planning to do and had marked her to die. I tried to convince her the best thing she could do was to talk to me, but . . ."

"They got to her first."

"That's what it looks like to me," Deirdre said. Kate's beeper sounded again, the noise high-pitched and harsh.

"Okay, now I'm really outta here," she said. She rose. Angel started to do the same. Kate waved him back. She looked at Deirdre, her expression serious. "I'll expect you to stay in touch."

"Yes, ma'am," Deirdre promised.

"That's yes, ma'am, Detective," Kate said. Then she disappeared into the outer office. Angel heard her voice, raised slightly in greeting, just before the door closed.

"Cordelia must be back from her errand run," he said to Doyle. "Why don't you—"

Before he could finish, Cordelia Chase burst through the door, her arms full of office supplies. Her purse was perched precariously on top of several reams of paper.

"Angel," she said, her voice urgent. "There's something I've got to—"

"I'm with a client, Cordelia," Angel said. "Not now."

"But I— Wait, did you say *client?*" Cordelia said. She peered around her armload of parcels. "*Client* as in *paying client?* I just saw a police-woman out there. I hope this isn't some sort of doing-her-a-favor type job."

"Actually . . ." Angel said.

Deirdre smiled at Cordelia. "Of course not."

Cordelia's frown cleared. "Great. Because, as Angel's office manager, let me tell you, he takes on way too many of those. The fact that he does good deeds hardly makes us a charity organization. I mean, I ask you, did you see the words not-for-profit on our business card?"

"Actually, I've never seen one of your business cards," Deirdre said.

Cordelia brightened even further. "Hold on," she instructed. "I'll get you some. You can hand them out to all your friends."

She took a staggering step toward the table.

"Cordelia, wait—let me—" Doyle began. But

it was already too late. The mountain of packages tilted, then toppled over. Cordelia's bag landed upside down, its contents shooting every which way. Something rolled across the table and tumbled off to land at Deirdre Arensen's feet. She stooped to pick it up.

"Don't touch that!" Angel shouted jumping to his feet.

Deirdre straightened, her expression puzzled. "All right. Keep your shirt on."

Angel rounded the table, dropped to his knees. "Where is it? Where did it go?"

In response, Deirdre opened one hand, right at Angel's eye level. Something that looked like an old coin rested in the center of her palm.

Angel met her eyes squarely. "What part of *don't touch that* didn't you understand?"

An expression of irritation crossed Deirdre's face. "Look, I thought we settled this. Just because I said I'd follow your instructions if I was in danger doesn't mean you can boss me around the rest of the time."

"You were in danger," Angel said as he came around the desk. "Are in danger."

"Since when?"

"Since the moment you picked that thing up."

"This?" Deirdre said, her tone incredulous. She grasped it between one thumb and forefinger and held it aloft. "I'm in danger because of this old coin?"

"Uh-oh," Doyle muttered under his breath.

"I tried to tell you," Cordelia said.

"Is that the one?" Angel asked, his eyes still on the object Deirdre was holding up.

"Looks like," Doyle acknowledged. "Of course, I'd have to get closer to be absolutely certain."

He stayed right where he was.

"Looks like what?" Deirdre asked. "What are you guys talking about?"

Slowly Angel turned around to face Cordelia. "Okay, Cordelia, where did it come from?"

"My next-door neighbor," Cordelia said.

"Oh, man, I knew that building was bad news," said Doyle.

"Which must be why you took me there in the first place," Cordelia countered.

Deirdre's eyes went from one to the other as if she were watching Olympic Ping-Pong.

Angel held up both hands. "Could we please just focus here, guys? How did you get it from your neighbor?"

Cordelia began to stuff her belongings back into her purse. "I stopped at my apartment before I came back here," she said in a slightly injured tone. "There was some stuff I wanted to drop off. You know that apartment next to mine has been empty practically forever and—"

"Just tell me how you got it, Cord."

"Well, I was *trying* to be friendly," Cordelia answered, closing the zipper on her purse with a vicious sound. "I saw this girl and she was carrying a box that was obviously too big for her. I looked for some burly moving guy to help, but they're never around when you want one."

"Sort of like traffic cops," Deirdre commented.

Cordelia brightened. "Exactly. So I thought, random act of kindness. Way overrated, let me tell you. First she drops the box right on my foot. It tips over and all her stuff comes rolling out. And *then* she expected me to help her pick it up!

"*That*"—Cordelia gestured to the object in Deirdre's hand—"was the last thing that I touched. But when I tried to give it back, it was like I suddenly had the plague or something. She backed up into her apartment and practically slammed the door in my face. And that was when I remembered that Doyle—"

"Had just been saying he was looking for this particular coin for his *collection,*" Angel cut in.

"My collection," Doyle nodded slowly. "That's it. I collect coins. All the time. Also, I give them away."

"You guys are incredible," Deirdre said. "Not to mention very bad liars."

Slowly she lowered her arm. But she kept ahold of the object under discussion.

"Trust," she said to Angel softly. "Didn't you tell me that was step one?"

"It's an amulet," Angel said. "Actually, it's a sort

of amulet in reverse. It summons evil, instead of warding it off."

"Generic evil, or specific evil?"

"Specific," Angel responded.

"And the specific evil it summons would be?"

"A fire demon by the name of Feutoch."

CHAPTER NINE

Terri Miller sat on the floor in the very center of her apartment, staring at the closest white wall. The apartment was perfect. Exactly what she'd wanted. Built in the Mission style, as if in tribute to old California. For some reason Terri couldn't explain, it made her feel like a part of life here. As if she'd always belonged. And if she belonged, didn't that mean that she was someone?

I should be happy, she thought. Perhaps compared to some others she hadn't asked for much, but the Illuminati were delivering exactly what they'd promised. Terri had a new life literally overnight. A beautiful apartment, filled with beautiful things. A new car. A new job. An address book filled with the names of "friends" she hadn't known she had.

She should be ecstatic. But she wasn't.

Because, as she gazed around her, she didn't

111

really see her new apartment. All she saw was the face of the girl next door. A striking face, the kind that didn't just belong to someone Terri might like to be, but to someone she might like to know.

It wasn't going to happen now. Because, whoever she was, the girl next door wasn't going to live that long.

Terri dropped her face into her hands. The fact that, even to her, her reaction felt obvious didn't render it any the less potent. *Dear God,* she thought. *What have I done?*

Joy Clement had tried to tell her, but she hadn't listened. Hadn't known how to listen, she realized now. Because never in her wildest dreams could she have imagined, in that moment, that the true price of becoming an Illuminati would be another human life.

Or more precisely, death. Her life for another's. That was the bargain. The package deal they'd offered. Her new life would rise from the ashes of a death by fire. Terri had thought they were joking at first. Or putting her through some sort of weird initiation ritual. Like a fraternity hazing.

You want to be one of us? First we have to see how far you'll go.

And had she hesitated, even when she'd understood that they were deadly serious? No, she had not. She hadn't thought about all the deaths that had gone before. All the ones that might be to come. Instead, she'd reached for the shiny brass ring of her dreams with both hands.

She'd taken the thing they called the Mark.

Why not? she'd thought. Proving she was worthy of being an Illuminati sounded so simple. So bloodless. All she had to do was pass the Mark on.

Sitting on the floor, her face still in her hands, Terri began to rock from side to side.

She could give it to anyone, they'd told her. Someone she knew and wanted to strike back at. A stranger on the street. Anyone at all. After that, it would be out of her hands. There would be nothing more for her to worry about. She'd have passed the test.

Tag, you're it. You don't know it, but your death's been summoned.

Even as part of her had recoiled in horror, Terri had shut those feelings down. She couldn't afford to think that way. Those feelings were a part of her old life. Where had they gotten her? What she needed was a transition, a new way of thinking. The change in perspective Andy had told her about. The Illuminati were providing her with the perfect opportunity to do just that. Pass on the Mark.

Why should she worry about other people? Hadn't they always ranked her last? Put her down? But the Illuminati were offering her just the opposite. The chance to be someone. To belong. The Illuminati were offering her the chance to come first. Who better to start the process than Terri, herself?

Besides, people died every day. They had unforeseen heart attacks. Got run over by city buses. Were the victims of drive-by shootings. Had head-on collisions with drunk drivers. One death more wouldn't make much difference, not when it meant Terri could have the life she'd always dreamed of.

Didn't she deserve to have her dreams come true after all she'd been through? Of course she did, the Illuminati had told her.

But they hadn't told her how she'd feel right this moment.

They hadn't told her how it would feel to look into someone else's eyes and know they were going to die. Because of you. Because of something you had done. Staring into the face of the girl next door, Terri had been horrified to see the truth.

Joy Clement had been right. The price the Illuminati required was too high. And, like Joy, Terri knew her realization had come too late. There was nothing she could do about it. The Mark had been passed on.

It wasn't until Terri felt the moisture, trickling out from between her fingers to dampen the cuffs of her blouse, that she realized she'd begun to weep. Her mind repeating the same litany, over and over.

I didn't know. I didn't see. I'm sorry. I'm sorry. I'm sorry.

Terri was gone, and Septimus couldn't find her.

He'd been loitering near the front of her building for a couple of days. The only time he left it was to do his regular Dumpster runs for food, or to see if Terri was at the grocery store. Finally, as his agitation over her absence increased, he'd stopped doing even that. Fearing to leave her apartment building unwatched, even for a moment. It wasn't like Terri to avoid him.

Where was she? Was she in some kind of trouble?

"Hey, you!" a voice snarled. "I see you. Get away from there."

Septimus started, then turned to see a heavyset man in a pair of stained blue coveralls bearing down on him. Mr. Taylor, the apartment building manager. He'd threatened Septimus before. Usually, Septimus did his best to avoid him.

"You got no business hanging around my front door," Taylor said. "I catch you here again, I'm calling the cops."

Septimus was feelng desperate. Otherwise, he'd never have been so bold. "Where is she?" he asked. "Where's Terri?"

A sneering expression appeared on the other man's face. "Oh, I get it. You're looking for your little girlfriend." Terri's kindness hadn't gone unnoticed. "Well, I got bad news for you," Taylor said. "Moved out. Left no forwarding address. You ask me, she couldn't take life in the big bad city anymore, and she's running back home to the folks."

"I didn't ask you," Septimus said.

Hot red color flooded Taylor's face. He took a step forward. "Don't you mouth off to me, you good-for-nothing asshole," he said. "I can get to you, anytime. Don't think I can't. I know where your little cardboard castle is."

Septimus took a sidling step back.

"That's right. Run away like the little splat of chicken shit you are," the other man taunted.

Septimus turned, and took off down the street. He wouldn't be back. Not because of Taylor's threats, but because there was nothing more for him here. Septimus didn't think Terri had gone home. She'd told him once that was the one thing that she would never do. They didn't understand her there, she'd said. A thing Septimus could definitely relate to.

Appearances might suggest otherwise, but Septimus thought he understood other people. He knew they didn't just disappear. People had habits. They had routines. Sure, they sometimes wanted something new. But they always came back to what was familiar.

He'd try the obvious places first, he decided, as he rounded the corner and slowed to a walk.

Right after he found himself a new place to sleep. Some guys slept pretty much anywhere, but Septimus wasn't like that. He always liked to establish a home base. A place he could come back to. One where he knew that he was safe. Once he'd done that, he'd start to search for Terri.

He'd find her. He had to, Septimus thought, as his heart began to beat uncomfortably fast. He couldn't let Terri go.

She was the one and only friend he had.

"I knew it," Deirdre Arensen said.

"Knew what?" Angel asked.

"My father—he said the cult members actually believed there was a fire demon." She gave a quick, self-conscious laugh. "I half had the sense that he believed in it, too."

"Well, duh," Cordelia spoke up suddenly. "Why have a fire-demon cult if there's no demon?"

"Lots of reasons," Deirdre said. "Whatever their mythical origins, cults generally exist to enhance the power of a cult leader. A *human* leader. If every reason for a cult's existence was based in fact, we'd all be putting plastic bags on our heads and waiting for the spaceships to touch down."

"Gross," Cordelia said.

"You told the police you thought the arsonist was a fire demon?" Angel asked.

Deirdre Arensen made a face. "Not exactly.

What I said was that I thought the cult existed and that its members were carrying out the murders believing they were doing a fire demon's bidding. His will. Whatever. A scenario like that could account for the way the profile makes no sense. You don't have one killer, you have an undetermined number of connected killers, all with the same intent."

"Not a bad explanation," Angel commented.

"The detective in charge didn't think that. No sooner had I said the words *fire-demon cult* than he was booting me out on my ass. I tried to tell him I thought I knew who the next victim would be—or one of the next victims. That was when he accused me of attempting to impede his investigation and threatened to have me arrested. But I can't help thinking . . ."

"If he'd listened to you, Ellen Bradshaw might still be alive?"

Deirdre nodded.

"All the more reason for you to listen to me now," Angel said.

Deirdre's eyebrows rose. "How do you figure that?"

"You said your research talked about a way for cult members to target a victim, to mark them for death." Angel gestured to the object Deirdre still held in her hand. "I'm saying that's it. It's called the Mark of Feutoch. As long as it's in your possession, you're a target. That's what summons the demon. When he shows up, you're dead."

"How come you know all this?"

"You're not the only one who can study the supernatural," Angel said. "I started out collecting incunabula, then sort of branched out."

"Is that legal?" Cordelia broke in.

"Cord," Doyle said.

"I just want to know if we should expect a late-night visit from Policewoman," Cordelia protested. She nodded in Deirdre's direction. "After all, she's practically her best friend."

Angel went to a shelf along one wall and pulled down a heavy volume, bound in leather. He returned to the table, opened it, turning pages swiftly until he came to what he was looking for.

"There," he said, turning the volume around to face Deirdre. "There it is."

In the center of the left-hand page was a drawing of what appeared to be a coin. The illustrator had been thorough. Both sides were shown in full detail. One side depicted a single, lidless eye, staring straight out. The other, a ring of fire. Beneath the second sketch was a series of numbers. One through seven.

"What do the numbers mean?" Deirdre asked.

"Those are all the possible numbers that can appear within the ring of fire," Angel answered. "It's called the time allowed. Essentially it's a countdown. The number tells how many days you've got before the demon comes for you, unless you get yourself off the hook by passing the Mark on. After that, it's somebody else's problem."

Without comment Deirdre slipped the Mark into her jacket pocket and turned the page. Once again, there were two illustrations, side by side. Deirdre pointed to the drawing on the left.

"That's him, isn't it? That's Feutoch?"

Doyle and Cordelia moved to peer over her shoulder.

"I told you these guys were trouble," Doyle said.

The illustration was of a pillar of flame. Within it, what looked eerily like a human outline was plainly visible. There were arms, legs, a head.

"That," Angel said, jabbing a finger at the illustration on the right, "is what happens to Feutoch's victims."

It was a drawing of a woman being burned alive. Her body consumed by the pillar of flame. In the illustration, the humanlike figure had his arms around her. Trapping her in a fiery embrace.

"Yuck," Cordelia said.

Deirdre was silent for a moment, one finger tapping against the tabletop. "Okay, so we know about what happens to the victims. What's in it for the cult members?" she asked.

In response, Angel turned the page again. There were no illustrations here, just tightly spaced script.

"Think of Feutoch as the fairy godmother from hell," he said. "Essentially, he promises to give his followers the lives they've always dreamed of. In exchange, each one targets an innocent victim for death."

He pointed to a particular line of text. " 'For everyone whose life is changed, a life is also forfeit,' " he read.

"So, cult members get the lives of their dreams. What does Feutoch get out of all this?" Deirdre asked.

"Lives," Angel answered. "Or maybe I should say deaths. He's doing a head count. When he reaches his target number, he'll be able to manifest all the time."

"Can't he do that now?"

"Nope," Angel said. "He has to be summoned. Called into being in this world. The one who does that is known as the Summoner."

"The cult leader, right?"

"Actually, wrong. It's more complicated than that. The cult structure is sort of two-tiered. The Summoner calls the demon into being. But, according to the book, it's a subordinate who actually sets up the cult. Converts the first members. Establishes the rituals. When things are up and running, he gets his reward."

"Don't tell me," Doyle put in. "They off him, right?"

"Got it in one," Angel said. "In exchange for all this help, the subordinate becomes one of Feutoch's victims."

"So no one in the cult knows the Summoner's identity," Deirdre broke in, her tone excited. "And *that* explains why the cult can die out, then resurrect itself. Even if the whole rank and file were to be wiped out, the Summoner would live on. The way to call the demon into being would still exist."

Angel nodded. "Which leaves us with a problem. It won't be enough to find and neutralize the cult. We've got to neutralize the Summoner."

"Or Feutoch," Deirdre said.

"Or that."

"How much time do we have?"

"What's the number on the Mark of Feutoch?"

Slowly Deirdre drew the Mark back out of her pocket and set it, ring of fire side up on the table. In the center of the ring was the number three.

"That's it, then," Angel said. "We've got three days." Seventy-two hours. It wasn't very much time.

Angel made a move as if to pick up the Mark. Deirdre snatched it back up and stuffed it in her pocket.

"I think you should give that to me," Angel said.

"Forget it," Deirdre answered shortly. She held up a hand when it was plain Angel was going to continue. "We've only got three days. That doesn't give us time to argue, and even if it did, you aren't going to win. I got my father into this, and it cost him his life. *I will not be responsible for anyone else's death.*"

As if forestalling further argument, Deirdre stood and snatched her purse from the back of her chair. She reached into a front compartment, pulled out a plain white business card, and tossed it down on top of the research book.

"That's how to reach me," she said. "If I come up with anything, I'll let you know. And I'll expect you to do the same. Trust, remember?"

"I remember," Angel said.

Without another word Deirdre strode from the office, the outer door closing with a bang behind her. A moment of silence filled the conference room.

"Well, that went well," Angel said.

Doyle moved Deirdre's business card aside so he could flip back to the page with the illustrations of Feutoch. "What didn't you tell her?" he asked.

Cordelia paused in the act of picking up the business card. "Wait a minute. You mean there's more?"

"Isn't there always?" Doyle answered.

"What is it this time?" Cordelia demanded.

"Things could get a little hot around here," Angel said. "When Feutoch gets his head count, he won't have to wait around to be summoned. He'll be able to manifest all the time, at will. The world will become his. A world of hellfire and brimstone. The inhabitants of the earth will perish or be made slaves. Only the followers of Feutoch will be spared."

"In other words, the end of the world," Doyle said.

"Oh, for crying out loud!" Cordelia exclaimed. "Not *that* again!"

Angel shrugged. What could he say? The concept was popular in certain circles. "Sorry," he said.

"So what's the plan? We do have a plan, don't we?" Cordelia asked.

"See if you can get anything out of your next-door neighbor," Angel said. "Stands to reason she's a new cult member. She's the only lead we've got, so don't scare her off. But we've only got a few days, so don't go too slow, either."

"Gee, anything else?" Doyle asked.

"When I know, you will."

"What will you be doing?"

"Trying to find a way to douse the fires of hell."

CHAPTER TEN

"Hello, Deirdre."

The sight of a figure crouching in the shadows by her front door had Deirdre Arensen jolting back a step before she could help it. A thing that definitely annoyed her.

Come on, Arensen. Get a grip.

Then the figure straightened, the hall light shining down onto its face. Deirdre added embarrassment to the mix. Naturally, it had to be him.

"Since when are we on a first-name basis?" she asked, moving forward aggressively. Detective Tucker held his ground a moment, then stepped back. Deirdre thrust her key into the lock but didn't turn it. Instead, she turned to face Tucker, her back against the apartment door.

"What are you doing here? Slumming?"

"Look, can't we just play nice for once?"

"I wasn't the one who started playing dirty," Deirdre said.

"You could invite me in," Detective Tucker suggested, with the hint of a smile.

"Bet that works nine times out of ten," Deirdre commented. "Unfortunately for you, I'm the tenth."

"This was on your mat." He held out a large manila envelope. DEIRDRE ARENSEN was written in bold, black letters across the front. There was no return address. And there weren't any stamps.

Deirdre tore it open. It was an excuse to keep him out in the hall, if nothing else.

Inside the envelope was a single sheet of paper. Taped to the front of it were a series of newspaper photos, all depicting her father's grisly death. Across the bottom, cut from single letters of newsprint, was a message:

Stop asking questions or you will be next.

Deirdre felt her breath hitch. She made herself count to ten before holding the page up, making sure her hand was steady as her eyes met Tucker's. She would not let him see that something like this had the power to shake her. Not the threat so much as the pictures of her father. She hated looking at how he'd died.

"How long has this been going on?" Detective Tucker asked.

"This is the first," Deirdre said. "What'd you do? Bring it with you?"

Tucker reached out to grasp her elbows in a tight, hard grip. "Just stop it, will you?" he said. "This is serious and you know it."

Deirdre forced herself not to look down at the images of what had happened to her father.

"It was serious before, or hadn't you noticed?" she shot back, and felt his grip tighten. "Wait," she blurted out. "Okay, wait, I'm sorry. I just—let go, all right?"

To her surprise, he did as she asked. Deirdre turned back to her apartment door, twisted the key in the lock, heard the satisfying *clunk* as the deadbolt shot back.

She opened the door, stepped into the entry hall, then turned back. She could see Tucker's eyes, watching her assessingly.

"Looks like I'm inviting you in after all, Detective."

"So, why did you come?" she asked a few moments later. She'd opened the windows to catch the breeze from the ocean. Gotten them both a bottle of mineral water. Tossed the envelope facedown on what had been her father's desk. She'd put the sheet of paper back inside.

Tucker was silent for a moment, staring out the window. "Something's come up," he finally replied. "I may need your help."

Deirdre gave a short bark of unamused laughter. "When will you know for sure?" she asked. She could see Tucker's jaw work as he bit back some sharp reply.

"I *do* need your help. I'm asking for your help," he said.

"You've got a hell of a lot of nerve, Detective. You know that?"

Tucker turned toward her, tried a grin. "Actually, I've been told it's one of my best qualities."

"By who? Your mother?"

Tucker's grin faded. "Okay, go ahead. Take a few more shots. I have them coming, I admit."

Suddenly exhausted, Deirdre flopped down onto the couch. "I'm beginning to get the way you operate," she observed. "If at first you don't succeed, try, try again."

Tucker moved to perch on the arm of the couch. "Look, I was a total jerk before. I know it, and I'm sorry. I apologize."

Deirdre huffed out a breath. "Boy, you really must be desperate."

Tucker leaned closer, his eyes intent. "I want this guy, Deirdre," he said. "I think you can help me catch him."

Deirdre took a sip of mineral water, concentrating on its cool, smooth glide down the back of her throat. How had this happened? She set the bottle of water on the floor at her feet.

"You didn't used to think so," she said.

Tucker began to pace around the living room, as if he couldn't stand sitting still.

"We finally located Ellen Bradshaw's next of kin, her mother and father."

Deirdre winced. She wondered how long it would take before she no longer had Ellen's death on her conscience.

"How'd they take it?"

"Like they'd been hit by a truck," Tucker said. "But there was something funny. You could tell they were stunned, but it was also like they'd been expecting it, or something. During the interview, her father left the room for a moment. The mother took the opportunity to tell us she thought her daughter had gotten mixed up with something strange. Something that had worried Mrs. Bradshaw and her husband. She didn't actually use the word *cult*—"

"But you think that's what she meant."

"I think I have to face the fact that it's a strong possibility," Tucker acknowledged. "Unfortunately, once her husband came back, Mrs. Bradshaw stopped talking. I got the impression the subject was taboo as far as the husband was concerned. We're trying to arrange a time to interview the mother in private. Meantime—"

"Meantime, the subject of cults is suddenly of interest," Deirdre filled in. "And you'd like to know what's in my father's files."

Tucker stopped pacing and flashed the smile. "I never said you were stupid."

"No, I think the term you used was *wacko*."

"Anybody ever tell you you ought to let bygones be bygones?"

"Nobody I'd still respect in the morning."

Abruptly Deirdre got to her feet and went to stand at the window. Her father had loved this apartment. The view straight out at the water. They'd even laughed about it. Martin Arensen had acknowledged the cliché, but the truth was, he'd loved the restlessness of the ocean. Never still. Always changing. Like the human mind, he'd told her.

But even though her eyes were on the sea, all Deirdre Arensen saw was fire.

It was in the way the sun sparkled on the waves, the way it reflected back from the windows. It had been there in the glare of the polished chrome trim of the car in front of her as she'd driven home from Angel's office. In the way the heat had seemed to shimmer up from the sidewalk as she'd walked to the apartment.

Everywhere she turned, no matter where she looked, Deirdre saw the thing that had killed her father.

Did she truly believe in the existence of a fire demon? She honestly didn't know. What she did believe was that, actual demon or not, there was a human agent involved. A mastermind. Someone who had set the whole thing up and pulled the strings from the background.

Which was worse? she wondered. An evil demon, or a human being so evil, so powerful, he could convince others of something that didn't exist? And in the name of that something, command others to do his killing for him.

"Look, I know you think I'm an egotistical asshole," Tucker's low, tight voice broke into Deirdre's thoughts. "It doesn't matter. All that matters is that I want what you want."

"And what would that be?" Deirdre asked. All of a sudden, she realized how tired she was.

"I want justice for the victims," Tucker said. "For Ellen Bradshaw and your father. If you know something, then you have to help me, Deirdre. Hate my guts if you want. But give me what you know. Help me catch this sicko bastard. Help me make the killing stop."

It was a hell of a sales pitch, Deirdre thought. She'd probably be a fool to trust him. If ever she'd seen ruthless determination, not to mention rampant ambition, in the flesh, it came in the form of Detective Jackson Tucker.

And am I any less determined? Deirdre thought. Hadn't she sworn a vow to do whatever it took to bring her father's murderer to justice?

Abruptly she spun on her heel and walked to the desk. Opening the bottom drawer, she removed a handful of hanging files.

Whatever it takes, she thought. She held the files out.

"You can start with these, Detective Tucker."

"Okay," Doyle said. "So, what have we got so far?"

He and Cordelia were on their way to her apartment. Because time was of the essence, Angel had loaned them his car. Doyle and Cordelia were trying to formulate a plan of action for getting to know Cordy's new next-door neighbor as they drove along.

"We knock on the door," Cordelia offered.

It was about as far as they'd gotten.

"Then what?" Doyle asked.

Cordelia took a corner with a squeal of brakes. "Then we . . . act spontaneous," she said brightly. "I mean, Angel's always telling us we should learn to think on our feet, right?"

"Right," Doyle agreed. Privately he had the feeling the boss would have liked a more concrete plan than this. Though even Angel had acknowledged he was assigning them a tall order. Get a stranger to trust you enough to give up her most important secrets in three days or less.

Cordelia accelerated through a yellow light. "The end of the world. I still can't get over it," she said. "I thought I'd left all that stuff behind when I left Sunnydale. I mean, once is enough for some kinds of things, don't you think?"

"Absolutely," Doyle said.

"And what is it with demons, anyway?" Cordelia asked, smacking the steering wheel for emphasis. "Those guys are always causing trouble. Talk about a pain in the—"

"Cord," Doyle interrupted. "I think this one's red."

"Okay, okay, no need to backseat drive. I see it," Cordelia said. She hit the brakes, bringing the car to a stop with a shriek. Doyle felt his seat belt strain.

"It's just that they piss me off," Cordelia said. "All they ever do is think about themselves, if you ask me. Getting other people to target innocent victims so you can bring about the end of the world. I mean, how selfish can you get?"

"Hey," Doyle felt obliged to protest. "This guy Feutoch's a pretty extreme case. They're not all that bad."

He was proud of the way he hadn't stumbled over the word *they*. Cordelia still didn't know that Doyle himself was half demon. It was pretty obvious it would be better for all concerned if things stayed that way. He still harbored secret dreams of a date, after all.

The light turned green, and Cordy hit the gas. "We're all set, right?" she asked. "I mean, because we're almost there."

"All set, right," Doyle said. "We knock on the door, and then we get spontaneous."

It was right about then that he realized he had a plain-old-run-of-the-mill-regular-old-fashioned-nonvision-related headache.

"Hi, I'm Cordelia, your next-door neighbor. And this is Doyle. We can come in, right?"

Doyle felt his headache kick up a notch. Cordelia's idea of spontaneous did not equate with subtle. Though he had to admit, it had its strong points. Cordelia wasn't just all talk. She also actually had her foot inside the door.

"Well, I—"

The new next-door neighbor sounded understandably reluctant. Doyle couldn't see her face clearly. The sunlight from the big windows the apartment boasted was strong and bright behind her, dazzling his eyes. She was mostly just an outline and a voice.

Wait a minute, Doyle thought. Through the headache he began to feel a stir at the back of his mind.

"Oh, hey, and if you're worried about that thing from earlier today, that coin thing, don't be," Cordelia said as she began to edge her way across the threshold.

"I don't have it anymore. I dropped my purse, and it must have rolled out somewhere. But that's okay, right?" she went on brightly. "I mean, you didn't want it back."

The new neighbor's hand jerked, pulling the

door open a little wider. "No, I didn't want it back," she said. Doyle could hear the relief in her voice. Perhaps it wouldn't be as hard as he'd feared to get this woman to confide in them, he thought. She seemed genuinely relieved that Cordelia was no longer a target.

Belatedly Cord's new neighbor seemed to realize that the question of whether or not to invite her unexpected guests in was moot. Cordelia was now actually inside the apartment. The woman pulled herself together, held the door open a little wider, backed up a couple of steps.

"I'm sorry. Won't you come in?" she asked.

Cordelia moved forward like a heat-seeking missile, aiming a look over her shoulder at Doyle. *Not bad, huh?* it said.

Doyle followed Cordelia into the apartment, his eyes quickly taking in the fact that it was pretty much a mirror of Cordelia's own. Though he assumed this one did not come complete with a roommate in the form of a ghost named Dennis.

"Nice furniture," Cordelia commented as she began to prowl.

"It's not mine," the other woman said. She moved to stand beside Doyle. He felt her quick movement of distress, quickly stilled. As if she realized she'd said something stupid and tried to snatch it back.

"I mean—the apartment came like this. Already furnished."

Doyle glanced over and saw her face clearly for the first time. Brown hair. Pointed nose and chin. Wide brown eyes that, in spite of her best efforts to the contrary, contained just the edge of alarm. She looked for all the world like a mouse trying to entertain two cats, Doyle thought. And felt the thing that had been trying to come to life in the back of his brain suddenly explode into being.

"Wait a minute," he said. "Don't I know you?"

"Oh, please," Cordelia protested. Having finished her scope of the living room, she moved on to the kitchen. "I have to apologize for him. He's not usually so lame," her voice sailed back through the door. "Though, actually, now that I think about it—"

"No, really, I mean it," Doyle protested. "The other night, in the grocery store. You helped me after I had one of my . . . attacks."

"Oh, right," Cordy's neighbor said. The information didn't seem to help any. She continued to look ever so slightly alarmed. It reminded Doyle unhappily of the lecture he'd given her. "So, you're okay?" she asked.

"Oh, yeah. As okay as I ever get."

Come on, idiot. Think of something. Keep the ball rolling.

Everything was starting to make sense now. The PTBs might have been slow, and, as far as Doyle was concerned, unnecessarily obscure, but they hadn't let Team Angel down after all. The final image, the one Doyle hadn't been certain was part of the vision or his return to the real world, had turned out to be both. They had their link to the cult, and knew who they needed to protect, all in one.

"So, you're Cord's new neighbor. Small world."

"Doyle," Cordelia said. She sailed in from the kitchen. Doyle wasn't certain he'd ever heard so much disapproval packed into just one syllable. Though, considering some of his previous exploits, maybe he had.

"I'm just going to go freshen up. You don't mind, do you?" Cordelia went on.

"Of course not." Her neighbor shook her head. Cordelia headed down the hall.

"Sorry to sound like a bad pickup artist. Guess I'm better at the lecture thing, huh?" Doyle said.

Cord's new neighbor turned back to him with a tentative smile. He could almost feel her begin to relax. Apparently, it was nice to see somebody else make a fool of themselves.

"I'm Terri—Terri Miller," she said. She extended her hand. Doyle shook it. Terri's grip was strong, but her fingers were cold.

"Good to meet you, officially that is. I'm Doyle—just Doyle—and that's Cordelia Chase. But then, I guess we sort of already said that."

Terri smiled again. Smiling changed her, Doyle

thought. Made her face softer, prettier. When she smiled, her face lost that desperate edge.

"I'm sorry. I'm not being a very good hostess. Would you like to sit down?" Terri asked. She gestured toward the couch, and Doyle sat down. Terri chose a chair just opposite him. She was facing the light now, the sun shining full on her features. *She looks . . . nice,* Doyle thought. *Too nice to be mixed up in something as ugly as this.*

"So, maybe we can get together sometime," he said. "A sort of welcome-to-the-neighborhood sort of thing."

For a fraction of a second, Terri looked genuinely surprised. Then she seemed to recover. "Sure, I guess. Do you live in the building, too?"

Doyle gave a quick, self-deprecating laugh. "Oh, no. Too rich for my blood. Cordy and I are co-workers. I was just seein' her home."

"That's thoughtful of you."

"Knight in shining armor, that's me."

"How about tonight?" Cordelia asked. She emerged from the hall and plunked down in a chair near Terri.

"What?" Terri asked.

"For that get-together," Cordelia said. "How about tonight? Right now. I mean, why waste time?" She shot Doyle a look.

"Time can be short," he seconded.

Cordelia nodded. "It can run out."

Terri's head swiveled between them as if she were watching a tennis match.

"But, hey—no pressure or anything," Cordelia added.

"Right," Terri said.

"Right we're coming on too strong, or right you'll go?" Doyle asked.

That remark earned Terri's biggest smile to date. "Right, I'll go. Can you guys give me a couple of minutes?"

"Sure," Cordelia said at once. She stood up. "Just come on over when you're ready. We'll be right next door. Don't bother to get up. We can find our own way out."

Seizing Doyle by one arm, she pulled him up from the couch and steered him toward the apartment's front door.

"See you in a few," Cordelia called as she opened the door and stepped out into the hall. Doyle followed, closing the door behind him. In silence the two walked the short distance to Cordy's apartment.

"I think she liked you," Cordelia said as she unlocked her own door.

A pained expression flickered across Doyle's face. "Could you possibly work on saying that without sounding so surprised?"

Cordelia considered for a moment. "I can try." She tossed her bag onto a table as Doyle followed her inside. "It still leaves us with one question, though, doesn't it?"

"And that would be?"

"Did she like you enough?"

I've done it, Terri Miller thought.

She'd had a regular conversation with regular people. People who'd liked her enough to ask her to go out. And she could say yes, because she no longer had to feel guilty. The girl next door, Cordelia, wasn't going to die. Wasn't going to be the one who paid for Terri's new life. The person who did that would be nameless, faceless. Terri herself was no longer directly responsible for what would happen because she hadn't been the one to pass on the Mark.

Without warning, a sensation of relief swept over Terri, so strong she felt almost giddy. What had she been so upset about? She had the life she'd always wanted. All she had to do now was to live it.

Starting right now.

Filled with determination, Terri dashed into the bedroom and slid open her closet door. In it hung a brand-new wardrobe, a thing she'd discovered during her explorations the night before. The clothes were perfect: simple, yet stylish. The materials, first-rate, in soft colors that wouldn't overwhelm her.

She knew exactly the dress she wanted. Silk, in a shade that was a pale reflection of Doyle's blue eyes. Terri got it out, laid it on the bed, then went to the bathroom to wash her face. Like everything else in the house, this room, too, was fully stocked. Jars bearing the label of Terri's favorite brand of cosmetics, the one she'd never been able to afford, sat on the counter.

If only Mama could see me now, she thought.

She ran warm water into the sink, splashed her face, then, eyes still closed, groped for a towel. Terri felt her questing fingers brush against one of the bottles on the counter, heard it topple over. With a crash it fell to the floor. Terri's eyes flew open.

Oh, no!

The impact shattered the bottle, shooting glass and expensive lotion across the bathroom floor. Horrified at what she'd done, Terri snatched up several pieces of tissue and knelt to clean up the mess.

Ouch! She straightened abruptly, a sharp fragment of glass protruding from her thumb. Terri pulled it out. Bright red blood welled up and splashed down, its color startling against the white of the sink. Terri rinsed her hand, then applied pressure.

What happens to all the blood inside your body when you're burned alive?

With a sound of dismay, Terri put her thumb between her teeth and bit down, hard. Where had that thought come from? She couldn't think like that. Wasn't going to think like that. That

141

kind of thinking belonged to the old Terri, the old life. But she didn't have to be that person, live that life anymore.

Taking her finger from her mouth, Terri whipped open the medicine cabinet and found a brand-new box of Band-Aids. She wrapped one around her thumb so tightly she all but cut off the circulation, then slammed the cabinet door closed. Her face appeared, reflected in the bathroom mirror. Pale. Strained. Terri watched, helpless to prevent it, as her eyes filled with tears.

"Oh, God."

Terri closed her eyes and let her head drop until her forehead rested against the cool glass of the mirror. All of a sudden, she felt completely exhausted, all her excitement of just a moment ago gone. In its place was a single question, circling like a shark in the back of her mind.

If her new life was being purchased with the life of another, just who, exactly, was the someone she'd become?

It's a good question, Doyle thought as he sat in Cordelia's living room, waiting while she changed her clothes. Every once in a while, Cordy got in a zinger, and it seemed she'd done so today.

Did Terri Miller like him enough? Enough to give up the life she'd always dreamed of to help him save the world? He certainly hoped so.

Without warning, Doyle felt a shiver slide

across his skin. *The life of one's dreams,* he thought. If someone offered him the same chance the Illuminati had offered Terri, what would he do? How far would he go to live the life he'd always dreamed of?

He wasn't so very different from Terri Miller. A thing he'd recognized about her as if by instinct that night in the grocery store. Doyle might tell himself he'd want a flashy car, and enough money so he never had to worry about a gambling debt ever again. But in his half demon/half human heart, he knew those things were just playthings compared to what he wanted most.

To not be different. To belong.

No wonder he'd felt an urge to protect Terri, he thought. She was an outsider, just as Doyle himself was. When offered the life of her dreams, she'd been smart. She hadn't pulled an Icarus. Reaching for something so high she'd be bound to crash and burn. She'd gone for something simple. The thing she'd always seen all around her yet always been denied.

A life like everybody else's.

I understand you, Terri Miller, Doyle thought. And because he did, for the first time he thought he understood the true power of the fire-demon cult. Not the promise of riches or fame, though members could choose those things if they wanted.

But the promise to grant the thing kept best

hidden, the thing most cherished, most longed for. The thing the outside world had denied most fervently. The innermost wish of a human heart.

Three days, Doyle thought.

That's how much time he had to persuade Terri Miller that what she'd spent a lifetime wanting wasn't worth it. Three days to convince her to trust him, even though it meant that she'd betray herself.

Doyle jolted as a knock sounded on the apartment door. Cordelia came out of the bedroom, fastening on a pair of earrings.

"You ready?" she asked, her tone serious.

Doyle rose. "As I'll ever be," he said. "Let's go."

CHAPTER ELEVEN

Angel drove the streets, the special radio he'd had installed tuned to the police band, the volume just barely audible. He'd been driving for hours. He could have stayed home and monitored police activity, but staying in his quarters felt too much like sitting around doing nothing. A thing he'd never been good at, even when he had time for it. Which he didn't, at the moment.

He'd tried telling himself he ought to be feeling more positive. Prospects of stopping Feutoch before he transformed the world into one great big giant red hot were definitely looking up. When Cordy returned the car earlier that evening, she'd confirmed that Doyle was out on a date with the girl next door. The three had started out together, but when Cordelia had realized how well Doyle and her new neighbor, Terri

Miller, were hitting it off, she'd left the field to him and headed back to the office.

She'd also relayed the news that Doyle had recognized Terri as being part of his original vision, thereby proving that the Powers That Be hadn't let Team Angel down after all. They'd just been more than usually unhelpful.

But even this information hadn't made Angel feel better. Instead, it had caused his anxiety level to ratchet up another notch. For the time being, Doyle had the point. There was nothing Angel could do. Not a situation in his comfort zone.

He turned a corner, not really paying attention to where he was going.

He had performed a few activities, such as beating the bushes at the usual demon haunts to see if he could turn up anything more on Feutoch. If any of the nasties he'd shaken down knew anything about the cult, or about the fire demon's overall time frame, they weren't talking. Hardly a surprise.

Lots of demons might not like the new living conditions that would exist when Feutoch ruled the earth, but they'd be all for the fact that he could do so. His coming would mean an end to human domination, a situation they considered unnatural, to say nothing of disappointing.

Angel braked at a red light, somewhat surprised to discover he'd driven to the La Brea Tar Pits, closest tourist landmark to the scene of the most recent death by fire. He drove the few blocks to the actual scene itself, parking across the street but leaving the engine on, letting it idle.

The police tape was gone. The mailbox had been repaired. Likewise the streetlight. Though that might be considered a mixed blessing, as it shone right down on the blackened sidewalk.

What was the name of the woman who died here? Oh, yes. Ellen Bradshaw.

What had she dreamed? What had she wished for that had been worth another human life? Angel wondered. And, most important of all, what had made Ellen Bradshaw change her mind about the Illuminati?

Angel got out of the car and went to stand on the black and pock-marked sidewalk. There had always been victims. Always would be. Some innocent. Some not. Angel knew that. But there was still something about the way the fire-demon cult got one set of victims to target another that seriously pissed him off.

The fact that cult members didn't think of themselves as victims didn't alter the fact that they were. They were dupes. Pawns. Sucked in by the oldest trick in the book. The promise of dreams come true.

Dreams come true, Angel thought.

Here was the hidden core of his uneasiness. The thing he really didn't want to think about much. If at all. Angel knew exactly what he'd wish for, if the Illuminati offered him their demon's bargain. And because he did, he knew how easy it would be to act on that wish. How small the step over the line that separated good from evil truly was.

Sure, he'd done some pretty terrible things back in the bad old days. But he hadn't been responsible in the way he would be if he did those same things now. He hadn't had a conscience then. He'd recognized but hadn't cared about the difference between right and wrong. Good and evil.

He couldn't care. He hadn't had a soul. In the two hundred plus years since he'd first been changed, Angel had probably never been closer to being truly human than he was right now.

And so he understood. Understood what it was to yearn. Understood what it was to want. The totally unattainable. The slightly out of reach. Anything it was possible to desire yet not possess. Anything at all. And because he did, he understood the true nature of what it was that he was up against.

Not just Feutoch, though that was bad enough. But human nature, as well.

It was the humans in the equation who kept the whole ball rolling. A human who summoned the demon in the first place. Humans who made the killings possible. They were just as guilty as

Feutoch, in Angel's view. And this was where the demon had been cleverest of all.

His human followers didn't have to do their killing face-to-face. They didn't have to look into their victims' eyes and see the spark of life snuff out. At the crucial moment the demon stepped in to do it for them. With each death he kept alive the illusion that his followers' new lives were free. That he could truly give them something for nothing.

But once in a while there's someone who gets it, Angel thought. Someone like Ellen Bradshaw. How many of Feutoch's victims over the centuries had actually been cult members? he wondered. Not that the demon was going to care. Each death only added to his overall head count.

Without his human accomplices, Feutoch was nothing but a lot of hot air. The big bad demon couldn't even show. But with them, he could become invincible.

Not if I have anything to say about it, Angel thought as he turned and made his way back to the car. He put it in gear, pulled away from the scene of Ellen Bradshaw's fiery death.

The question was, would Angel get to have his say in time?

It was taking too long.

He prowled his apartment, unable to settle. Unable to bear the fact that he was doing nothing. This way. The old way. It was taking too long. He wanted the change, and he wanted it now. He wanted the new world.

A world lit only by the fire of hell.

He opened the fridge, pulled out a beer. Twisted off the top, then slammed the bottle down on the counter. He didn't want a drink. He wanted action. Because there was something else that bothered him. A lot.

He took a swig of beer after all, enjoying the way it seemed to sear the back of his throat. He was the one who kept the ball rolling, wasn't he? Or maybe that should be, kept the Mark rolling. He was the one who recruited new cult members and, in so doing, upped the fire demon's head count. Feutoch would be up shit creek without a paddle if it wasn't for him. A fact that deserved a little recognition, a little respect.

Like, say, for instance, in the form of him being the demon's right-hand man. The human who'd reap the most benefit after the change. But was he that right-hand man? No, he was not.

He wasn't. The Summoner was.

He took another swig of beer as he made his way into his living room and began to pace. It was a big gyp. That's what it was. All the Summoner had to do was call forth the demon in the first place, then sit back and enjoy the ride.

The Summoner didn't have to constantly be on the watch, judging total strangers to see if they'd make good converts, the way he did. He hadn't made many mistakes, a thing that he was proud of. And the few he had, he'd handled quickly and effectively. The way he had with Ellen Bradshaw and Joy Clement.

He did all the work, the Summoner got all the glory. That pretty much summed the situation up in a nutshell. But the thing he hated most was that there was nothing he could do about it. No one with whom he could lodge a protest.

He didn't know who the Summoner was.

He knew that was the way it was supposed to work. The way it had always worked. That didn't mean he had to like it.

His lack of knowledge ate at him, like a cancer. The identity of the Summoner was a loose end, and loose ends were dangerous. They tripped you up when you least suspected. Snatched the victory trophy from your hands even as you reached for it. Loose ends meant your illusion of control was just that and nothing more.

He set the half-empty bottle of beer down on the coffee table as he contemplated his options. He could see only two. Let things stay the way they were. Maintain the status quo. Or change his perspective and thereby change the scenario.

What was the bottom line, after all? Feutoch wanted lives. It was his job to provide them. Why couldn't he speed things up? Do his job on his own timeline. He didn't think the demon would complain. Each life Feutoch took only brought him closer to his ultimate goal. The only person who might object was the Summoner. Because the tables would be turned. The Summoner would no longer have control.

Smiling now, he moved into the entry hall and shrugged into his jacket. If his actions brought the Summoner out into the open, so much the better, he thought. Anyone who could be seen could be a target. And targets were made to be brought down. If he could help Feutoch accomplish his goal at the same time he rid himself of a competitor, so much the better.

Pocketing his keys, he was whistling "Light My Fire" as he left the apartment.

"Hey, man, you wanna ride?"

Septimus put his head down and kept on walking. He knew better than to look up, or make eye contact. Better than to show he'd heard at all. He'd lived on the streets a long time. He'd been hassled before. Sometimes it felt as if he'd been the butt of jokes and harassment his whole life. Septimus Stephens, the easy target. The slow one.

"Come on, man, don't be like that," the voice sounded again. "We can help you find what you're looking for."

Against his better judgment, Septimus stopped walking. How had this guy known he was looking for someone? Still suspicious, he eyed the car. It was big and fancy. Foreign, he thought. In it, he could see three guys. Two in the front, one in the back. The guy in the front passenger seat was leaning out, the window down.

"I'm looking for Terri," Septimus blurted out. "Do you know where to find her?"

"Whoa—a babe hunt!" the guy in the backseat suddenly yelled.

"Shut up, Sam," the guy in the front seat said without even turning around. He gave Septimus an engaging smile, the sort of smile that made Septimus want to trust him.

"Terri, sure," he said. "I think I know her. Why don't you hop in? I bet together we could find her."

Septimus hesitated. He wasn't supposed to take rides from strangers. He knew that. It was one of the things his father had told him, over and over. But he was tempted now.

He put his hand in his coat pocket, feeling for the envelope. He'd put it there for safekeeping, even though it meant he'd had to fold it. He'd promised himself he wouldn't take it back out until he could show it to Terri. A sort of test of faith, of his will to find her. The thought of the way her eyes might light up with pleasure when she saw the animal stamps finally decided him.

"Okay," he said. "I'll go."

✷   ✷   ✷

"Evening, George."

"Good evening, sir," the valet parking attendant said, deciding instantly to give this guy his very best service. He definitely had "the look," George thought.

Angular, blond. Lean and ever so slightly dangerous. The look every woman in L.A. seemed to be so hot for. Of course, the sleek, black 'Vette he was currently climbing out of didn't hurt things, either. It would be a pleasure to drive that baby over to the lot. Maybe he'd have to take the scenic route, George decided.

"Take good care of her," the guy said, lobbing him the keys. "I'm trusting you now, George. In fact"—his voice lowered, became more confidential—"I could use your help with something."

"Happy to be of assistance, sir," George said, hoping he didn't sound too much like a brownnoser.

"I think she's been pulling a little to the right when I corner. Take the long way to the lot, will you? Tell me if you think she needs a trip to the shop. You drive a lot of cars. I figure you've got a good touch."

"Yes, *sir!*" George said. This was definitely starting to look like his lucky night. If this guy tipped as smooth as he talked, George just might add a nice little sum to his own car fund.

"Great," the guy said. "See you after dinner. What's good here, by the way?"

"Haven't a clue," George confided in his turn. "I can't afford it."

Come on, mate, Doyle told himself. *Let's get this show on the road.*

He looked across the table at Terri Miller, who was taking tiny sips of her white zinfandel. If Feutoch didn't get her, her choice of beverage would, Doyle thought. Though he'd have to be the first to admit his own tastes were hardly L.A. He was definitely a room-temperature Guinness man himself. Tonight he'd had to settle for some made-in-Oregon microbrew. A cold one.

"Too bad Cordelia had to go," Terri suddenly blurted out.

Doyle gave an inward wince. He was pretty sure Cordy had cleared out to give him plenty of room to work his charm. Unfortunately, it appeared as if the well of charm had run dry. The conversation with Terri had become stilted and awkward, a thing Doyle was beginning to attribute to his surroundings. He was never at his best in a fern bar.

Come on, he chastised himself now. *It's not as if you've got all the time in the world.* Or maybe that should be, it wasn't as if the world had all that much time.

"Yeah, it is too bad," he heard himself agreeing lamely. Cordelia's excuse had been that she'd been called back to the office. "We work kind of strange hours sometimes."

Terri took another sip of white zinfandel, her eyes on the tabletop. "What kind of work do you guys do?" she inquired.

"Oh, the usual thing," Doyle replied. "Fighting the powers of darkness, making the world safe for the everyday man and woman on the street."

Terri's hands jerked on the stem of her wineglass, causing some of the rosy liquid to slosh out onto the table.

"Hey, take it easy," Doyle said as he mentally kicked himself. Angel might know how to slip asking a girl to help him save the world into a casual conversation, but Doyle would be damned if he did. "Actually, it's pretty boring. We do, um, research for this sort of global think tank."

"You were joking," Terri said.

Doyle gave a self-deprecating snort. "Of course I was joking. Do I look like some kind of superhero?"

Terri's expression changed at once. "You shouldn't think that way," she said, surprising them both with her sudden vehemence. "You've got lots of great qualities. All you have to do is appreciate them for what they are. That's the only way other people will."

There was a tiny silence.

"Um, thanks," Doyle said. "I appreciate the vote of confidence."

Terri dropped her head down into her hands. "I was lecturing, wasn't I? I didn't mean to. I hate it when other people do that."

"Don't worry about it," Doyle said easily. "Hey, I had it coming, right?"

Terri lifted her head. Doyle could see the beginnings of a smile, hovering at the edges of her mouth.

"Even?" he asked.

The smile blossomed. "Even," Terri said. "I won't give you any advice about how to date, if you won't tell me not to take candy from strangers."

"Hey—I never said anything about candy," Doyle protested. "But for the record, my advice on that is—hold out for the expensive stuff. Any jerk can buy a bag of M&M's."

Terri laughed, her whole face lighting with amusement. Doyle felt his confidence surge, even as he experienced an unexpected twist in his gut. She was nice, he thought as he had in her apartment. Unpretentious. And so starved for attention that even his lame attempts looked good to her.

And what was he doing? Setting her up.

No, it was more than that. So much more complicated, he thought. He was literally trying to save the world, and the woman across from him was his best link to the thing that would come to destroy it. But that didn't mean he had to like the fact that destroying the evil would most likely also mean destroying a thing he thought he could learn to value: Terri Miller's trust.

Just do your job, he told himself.

"So, where'd you come from?" he asked, between sips of beer. "You're not from around here, are you?"

Terri grimaced. "Is it so obvious?"

"Of course not," Doyle said at once.

"Well, it's obvious *you're* not from here," Terri countered.

"No way. I'm from West Covina. Swear to God."

Terri laughed again. "I'm from Kansas," she acknowledged with a roll of her eyes. "I mean, really. How corny can you get?"

"Well," Doyle said. "You're certainly not in—"

"Another round?" The voice of the waitress sliced through the conversation.

"Sure," Doyle said. "Why not?" The longer they stayed, the better his chances.

"Same again?"

Doyle nodded. The waitress made a notation on her pad and sauntered off. "So, where were we?" Doyle asked.

"Telling how we ended up in L.A.," Terri supplied. She reached for her glass, downed the last sip of wine. "I lectured first, so you get to tell the story of your life first."

She's warming up, Doyle thought. With luck,

he could turn a chat about the good old days into the formerly not-so-good present ones. With luck.

"Actually," he said, "there's not much to tell. I ended up here because I got tired of living in a place where everybody thought they knew me. Don't you find that people who get all nostalgic over small towns never actually grew up in one?"

Terri nodded her head in agreement. "Uh-huh. Everybody watches you in a small town. But I figured, in a place as big as L.A. . . ." Her voice trailed off.

Doyle pulled in a silent breath. *Finally,* he thought. A genuine opening. Now all he had to do was to walk through it. "And how's it workin' out? I mean, I know from experience settling in here can be kind of tough. Finding a new set of friends, and all."

Terri made a vague gesture with her hand. "Oh, it's going all right. It was a little hard at first, but now . . ." She glanced at Doyle. "Finding the new apartment really helped."

Either he was really rusty, or she was trying to say she liked him. "I'm glad to hear it," Doyle said with a smile.

"One microbrew, one white zin," the waitress announced.

Doyle leaned back as she deposited the new drinks on the table and cleared the empty glasses. All of a sudden he realized he was starved. Pumping unsuspecting people for information really worked up an appetite.

"Can we see a menu?" he asked suddenly. He looked at Terri. "I'm getting kind of hungry, how about you?"

Terri blushed. "You don't—I didn't mean for you to have to take me to dinner," she stumbled.

Doyle tried a sheepish grin. "Hey," he said. "Don't shoot me down. I'm trying to be spontaneous and charming here."

The waitress cleared her throat, her impatience obvious. Terri's chin came up.

"I'm starved and I'd love to see a menu," she said.

Excellent, Doyle thought. Though, as he scanned the options on the piece of off-white parchment paper the waitress thrust into his hands, he made a mental note to beg Angel to give him an expense account.

He stepped inside the restaurant, senses alert. He could see the maître d' snap to attention at the far end of the foyer from the corner of his eye. That was when he heard it: the rev of the Corvette's engine, followed by a short squeal of tires. He'd known George wouldn't be able to resist the opportunity to really step on the gas. In fact, he'd counted on it.

He took a few steps toward the desk where the maître d' waited, then pulled up short, his hand going to the inside pocket of his coat. He pulled the beeper out, checked the number, then returned the unit to his pocket.

"Sorry, looks like I'll have to take a raincheck."

He spun on his heel, quickly retraced his steps.

"Sir," he heard the maître d' call behind him. "If I just might know the name of your party . . ."

He yanked the door open and let it slam closed behind him. Thrusting his hands into his pockets, he began to amble away down the street, feeling more than a little pleased with himself.

He'd take his time, see what was out there. But, eventually, he'd mark three tonight, he decided. He wouldn't get carried away. He'd just . . . flex his muscles. There were so many potential victims for Feutoch, after all.

And he'd make sure that each and every one he marked tonight had so little time.

CHAPTER TWELVE

"No, no," Septimus said. "We have to go back. This is all wrong."

They'd been driving for what felt like hours. But it hadn't been until they'd got onto the freeway that Septimus had started to feel alarmed. They were leading him away from Terri.

"We have to go back," he said again. "I know Terri. She wouldn't go this far."

"Just trust me on this one, all right, Septimus?" the guy in front, whose name was Doug, said. "Every babe in the world wants to go where we're going."

The car took an exit and began to cruise through a shopping district. It was all Septimus could do to keep from crying. The streets were immaculately manicured, filled with fancy restaurants and dressed-up shop windows. Terri would never come here.

"Let me out," he begged. "I want you to let me out."

Doug shrugged. "Whatever you say, buddy."

He made a gesture and the driver pulled over, bringing the car to a halt in front of one of the fancy stores. It was after closing, but the sidewalk was still full of people. They scattered like startled birds as Septimus hurtled from the back of the car.

"Hope you find your girlfriend," Doug said as he leaned over and slammed the door. "And hey—have a really nice life." He gave a snort of laughter. "But if I were you, I wouldn't count on it."

With a squeal of tires the car roared off, leaving Septimus standing alone. *It's all right*, he told himself. He could make this all right. The first thing was to get away from these bright, pristine streets where he stuck out like a sore thumb.

Putting his head down so he wouldn't have to see the way people crossed the street to avoid him, Septimus began to walk back the way he'd come.

"That's it?" Angel barked at Doyle.

Following his so-called date with Terri Miller, Doyle had reached Angel on the cell, and they'd arranged to rendezvous back at the office so Doyle could give Angel a full account. Doyle had spent most of his travel time trying to convince

himself there was a positive spin to an evening
that had actually come perilously close to being a
total bust.

Try as he might, Doyle had been unable to
shake a slightly sick feeling, one directly related
to the gut-level belief that, if Angel had been the
one to go out with Terri, he'd have gotten the information Team Angel so desperately needed by
now. Whereas about the only thing Doyle could
claim was that he'd managed to establish a good
rapport. Which wasn't bad as far as it went. The
trouble was, it didn't go far enough.

And then there was the major setback of the
evening: Terri had declined Doyle's invitation to
go out again the next night. She'd claimed she
had a previous engagement. One she couldn't get
out of. Doyle had figured out a positive spin for
that, too, but he hadn't gotten the chance to express it yet. It was hard to express opinions when
the boss was biting your head off.

"Drinks and dinner, for which you've just
stiffed me, and all you've got is that she won't go
out with you again tomorrow?" Angel said now.
"What's the matter? Losing your touch?"

"Hey," Doyle protested from his position on
the couch. It didn't help to have Angel telling
him the exact same things he'd already told
himself. "I never claimed I was some Casanova.
You were the one who said I shouldn't rush
things."

"Within reason. We've only got a couple of days, Doyle."

"I know that," Doyle answered, his tone growing testy. "I've been able to count for quite a while now."

Angel took a restless turn around the room. At the rate he was pacing, Doyle thought, there'd be grooves in the floor.

"Maybe she's just doing a girl thing, you know—"

Doyle shook his head. "Not her style. She's kind of—sweet."

Angel stopped in mid-stride and swung around. "Sweet," he echoed, his tone making it clear he was finding this more than a little hard to buy. "She's a follower of Feutoch. She marked Cordelia."

"I know that," Doyle said once more. "I'm not saying she's a total innocent, I'm just saying—"

"You like her," Angel interrupted. "You actually like her."

Buffy liked you, Doyle thought. Aloud he said, "Yeah, so?"

"So, maybe you're wrong about her motivation for turning you down. It's hard to keep your objectivity when you like someone."

All of a sudden Doyle had had enough. He shot to his feet. "Okay," he said. "I'm outta here."

"Hey," Angel said. "Don't get all bent. I just—"

"Want to make it perfectly clear that you think

I'm a total idiot," Doyle filled in for him. He stepped around the couch to face Angel directly. "You think that I can't handle this, don't you? That I'd let personal considerations get in the way of the big need-to-save-the-world-type picture. Well, you can just go to hell."

There was a potent beat of silence.

"Already done that," Angel answered softly.

Doyle snatched up his jacket and headed for the door. "Don't expect me in during the day. I'll check in tomorrow night."

"What for?"

Doyle pulled his jacket on with two quick, angry motions. "The reason Terri wouldn't meet me," he said evenly, "is that she has a meeting to go to. One she said she couldn't miss. I'm betting that it isn't Weight Watchers."

Angel made an exasperated sound. "Why didn't you say so before?"

"You didn't give me a chance," Doyle said. "You were too busy letting me know I wasn't holding my end up."

"Doyle."

Doyle stopped in the act of opening the door but didn't turn around. "What?"

"What time's the meeting?" Angel asked after a moment.

"Seven o'clock. I don't know how far away it is, so I figured I'd start watching Terri's place as early as five. I can trail her, see where she goes."

"Sounds good," Angel said.

"Thanks for the big, fat vote of confidence." Without looking back, Doyle stepped across the threshold. He was just about to pull the door closed behind him when the police radio blared to life.

George had decided to reward himself. Usually he went right home on weeknights. It was a long drive from the restaurant to where he lived over his parents' garage in Santa Monica. The only reason he'd taken the job in Beverly Hills in the first place had been because the guy who ran the valet service was a business crony of his father's.

But tonight George figured he had reason to celebrate. The guy in the black Corvette had come through big time. He'd slipped him a hundred-dollar bill, with a coin tucked into the very center. George hadn't recognized the coin, but he hadn't cared. The hundred was what he cared about. He could blow half of it and still have a decent amount to slip into his car fund.

Not that he intended to blow that much. But walking into one of those trendy bars in Beverly Hills where the bartender always looked at him as if he couldn't afford a glass of tap water and slapping that hundred down sounded like a pretty good time.

He had one beer, then two. It was after the

third that he realized it was almost midnight and he'd better head for home. His mom knew he never stayed out during the week. She was probably wearing a track in the living-room rug right now.

The floor of the bar wasn't quite as steady as it had been when George pocketed his change and headed for the door. The sidewalk misbehaved in the same fashion as George walked to his car. He made it to the parking garage just before it closed. It stayed open late on weekends, but during the week, it closed at midnight.

George got behind the wheel of his ancient Chevy, started the ignition, and pulled carefully from the lot. Deciding a little help staying awake was probably in order, he reached to switch the radio on. As he did so, he saw a strange flicker of movement in the passenger seat out of the corner of his eye. He turned toward it.

"What the—"

And then he was screaming, the car lurching out of control and up onto the sidewalk as he released the wheel and tried desperately to scramble from the car.

He never made it out. It was hard to manipulate a door mechanism when one's fingers were on fire, curling in upon themselves.

Septimus kept walking. He was tired. Hungry. But at least the streets were emptier now. Quieter. Darker. A thing that made him feel a little better. In the dark he didn't stand out so much. He paused on a street corner, considering which direction to go next. As he hesitated, a car pulled out of a nearby parking garage.

It wasn't a fancy car like the ones Septimus had been seeing for hours, like the one that had brought him here. This one looked older, more like the cars from the neighborhoods that Septimus was used to. *Maybe it's a sign,* he thought. Eagerly he watched the car. Unless it went back the way he'd just come, Septimus decided to go in whatever direction the car did.

The car made a left, continuing in the direction Septimus had already been going. He felt his spirits lift. He'd been doing it right after all. He was going to get out of here. He was going to find Terri. Everything was going to turn out fine.

Then, as he watched, the inside of the car exploded with light. With a squeal of brakes, it turned sharply, veering up onto the sidewalk. Septimus could see the inside.

It's on fire, he thought.

For one split second he could have sworn that he saw shapes within the flames. They looked for all the world like two lovers, locked in an embrace. Then there were no shapes at all. Only fierce, hot flames.

Septimus stood on the sidewalk, rooted to the spot. He could feel the heat, though his body broke out in a cold sweat. He knew what fire meant. Hadn't his father drilled it into him since the day he was born?

Eternal damnation. Everlasting hell.

The thing that would happen if you did wrong things. The place you would end up if you didn't make them right.

That was when he began to run. Around the car. Down the street. Not looking back. Away, away, away from the fire.

It wasn't until he heard the first sirens begin to scream across the night that he realized what he'd taken for them all along had been the sound of his own.

Angel watched as Doyle checked in the doorway, then whipped around as information began to stream into Angel's quarters over the police radio. Multiple units, fire engines, and aid cars were being summoned to Beverly Hills.

"The time," Doyle said, his voice strained. "Look at the time."

Angel turned to read the numbers on the digital clock that sat on a shelf beside the police radio.

12:01.

One minute into a brand-new day. And, unless Angel very much missed his guess, the old one had just ended with Feutoch adding another victim to his head count.

CHAPTER THIRTEEN

Detective Kate Lockley had had better mornings.

Usually halfway decent mornings were the result of halfway decent nights. Kate's most recent night had been downright lousy. She'd spent the majority of it on a stakeout in an unmarked squad car. An anonymous tip had claimed that the leader of the crack-cocaine ring the department had been trying to nail was holed up at a certain address in East L.A. It should have been a matter of just plain showing up, waiting him out, and making an arrest.

Kate and a partner had done the showing up and the waiting. The making the arrest part was the thing that hadn't gone so well. Either the guy had never been there in the first place, or the tip had been bogus. Now Kate had to file paperwork to that effect, in triplicate, before she could go home, shower, and catch a quick nap before heading back for her regular shift.

Though she had no one but herself to blame for that, she thought, as she stomped up the front steps. She'd offered to file the paperwork herself. If the guy she was working the case with got home right away, he'd be able to see his kids before they headed off to school for the day.

She pulled the front door open, greeted the uniform at the front desk, then made her way straight to the coffeemaker. It was a relatively new pot, she noticed. With luck, that would mean the battery-acid effect would be somewhat less than usual.

She hoisted the pot, filled a Styrofoam cup, and was just about to set the pot back down when Detective Tucker came around the corner. *Right up there on top of my Last Thing I Need list,* Kate thought. Her only consolation was that the Hick looked even worse than she did. But then she supposed he had better cause. Kate knew what had happened last night. It was likely every cop in the city did.

Deciding cop solidarity was more important than personal antipathy, she hoisted the pot in his general direction.

"Pour you a cup?" she inquired.

Tucker stopped short, scowling. "What'd you do? Poison it?"

"Do you think I need to?" Kate replied.

To her surprise, that earned her what looked to be a genuine smile. Tucker walked the remaining steps to the coffeemaker, then leaned against the wall beside it, for relaxation or support, Kate couldn't tell.

"You have a point, Lockley. Though if you tell anybody I said you were right about even that much, I'll publicly deny it."

"They'd never believe we could agree about anything anyway," Kate said. She set her own cup down and poured a second one. "Cream, sugar?" she inquired.

Tucker's eyebrows rose. "What's with the making nice, all of a sudden? You feeling all right?"

Kate plunked the pot back into position and kept a lid on her temper. She didn't like him any better, but she had to feel for the guy. The last person's shoes she'd want to be in were Tucker's this morning. Or actually, any morning. There were lots of things that weren't so rosy about being a cop, but in Kate's experience, none of them was worse than working a murder investigation that wasn't going well. Particularly when you were in charge, and the case was high profile.

Tucker probably had the mayor, the city council, and virtually every other elected official Kate could think of breathing down his thick, tanned neck. Not to mention the entire population of the greater Los Angeles area. She wouldn't wish that kind of attention on her worst enemy. It only made doing the job harder.

"I'm feeling fine," she said now. "But I could ask you the same question."

To her surprise, Tucker actually chuckled. "Well," he said as he straightened up and took the cup of coffee she'd poured. "Now that we've established mutual trust, I'd say we're well on our way to a meaningful dialogue. I may have to ask you out."

"Don't push your luck," Kate advised.

"Ouch," Tucker said. "That sound you hear is my ego hitting the floor."

Kate took a sip of coffee. "Funny," she said. "I'd have thought the sound would be a lot louder."

Tucker added artificial creamer to his coffee, stirred it in, took another sip, then added more. "So, Detective Lockley," he said. "What brings you in so bright and early in the morning?"

"I was on a stakeout all night," Kate said.

"I hope you caught the bad guy."

"Am I smiling?" Kate asked.

"Not noticeably."

"Then I didn't catch the bad guy."

"Too bad."

"We heard," Kate blurted out, surprising herself. "Over the radio. While we were sitting around doing nothing."

Tucker snorted. "I imagine the whole country's

heard by now." Without warning, he slammed the container of creamer down beside the coffeemaker. "Dammit!" he exploded. "This is impossible. Two months. *Two months!* And we still don't have anymore to go on than when we started. And if you mouth me some platitude about how these things take time, Lockley, I'm going to ram this little red stir stick right down your throat."

"Wouldn't dream of it," Kate said. "Red's not really my color."

Though, privately, she thought anyone who'd have been brave enough to put forward such an opinion would have had a good point. Killers like the Krispy Kritter weren't made in a day, and they weren't caught in one, either. Not that that helped much, when catching one was your job.

At her response Tucker shook his head. "Sorry." He lobbed the stir stick into a nearby wastebasket, then took a sip of coffee, his eyes assessing Kate over the rim of the Styrofoam cup.

"You don't rattle easily, do you Lockley? I can see why you and Deirdre are such great pals."

Kate paused, her own cup of coffee halfway to her lips. "What did you say?" she asked.

"Don't push it," Tucker growled. "I said I was sorry."

"No, the other thing," Kate pressed. "The one about Deridre and I being such pals. Since when are the two of you on a first-name basis?"

For the first time since she'd known him, Tucker seemed off guard. "Since yesterday, actually."

"Yesterday," Kate said. "Would that be the same yesterday that's just a couple of days after you chewed me out because you thought I was funneling information to her?"

"You *were* funneling information to her."

"You can't prove that."

"Look," Tucker said. "Something came up when I was interviewing Ellen Bradshaw's parents. Turns out they thought she'd been running with a pretty weird crowd."

"You mean a cult," Kate said.

Tucker nodded. "Yeah. Not that they said that right out. But it was pretty clear what they meant. That was when I remembered Deirdre—Dr. Arensen's—theory—"

"Harebrained theory," Kate corrected. "I think that's what you said."

Tucker glared.

"So what did you do?"

"I went over to her apartment and debased myself."

Kate pushed back an unexpected spurt of laughter. Boy, would she have loved to have been a fly on the wall during that conversation.

"Did it work?" she asked.

For a split second Tucker looked surprised. Kate could feel her face turn red. He'd assumed she'd known, she realized. That the flow of information between Kate and Deirdre went two ways. It should have. *Calm down, Kate,* she told herself. *You've been on duty for hours. There's probably a message waiting on your desk.*

"We're just old friends," she said, driven to defend Deirdre by some impulse she couldn't quite name. "We're not joined at the hip."

"All right," Tucker answered. "Keep your shirt on. As a matter of fact, it did. Work, I mean. She loaned me her father's files. I'm still going through them, but so far, they're not telling me much. Such as why all the murders occur at midnight. This last one's the strangest yet."

"The kid in Beverly Hills," Kate said.

Tucker nodded. "His car is toast. God knows why it didn't explode. Could be a break for us, though. Forensics is pretty sure the fire started *inside.*"

Kate's eyebrows went up. "You think he knew his killer, that he gave him a ride?"

"Maybe," Tucker said. "But if he did, how did the Krispy Kritter get out in time?"

"Maybe he got out earlier," Kate suggested. "But left something behind. Some kind of incendiary device."

"Of which there's absolutely no trace so far."

"Well, it's early yet, isn't it?" Kate asked reasonably. "There's still time for forensics to come up with something."

"You really are your father's daughter, aren't you, Lockley?" Tucker asked, his tone suddenly vicious. "I should have known you'd take the old-school cop line."

Kate jerked back as if he'd slapped her. *To hell with this,* she thought. *Why on earth did I bother to be nice?* Tucker was an asshole, through and through. When things didn't go his way, he looked for the first available target. It was just her bad luck she'd put herself in his way. Well, that was a situation she could rectify.

Kate downed the rest of her coffee in one bitter gulp. "For your information," she informed Tucker in a tone like ice, "I happen to be very proud to be my father's daughter. He's the one who taught me that integrity was important. Not that I'd expect you to understand the concept."

She crushed her coffee cup, lobbed it into the wastebasket, and set off down the hall toward her office.

"No, I'm not saying I think you did the wrong thing. I'm just saying I wish you'd told me, that's all."

It was several hours later, and Kate was back at her apartment. She'd had her shower, something decent to eat, but the nap she'd wanted was apparently not in the cards. Every time she got close to dropping off, Deirdre's and Tucker's faces floated inside her closed eyelids.

There'd been no message from Deirdre waiting on Kate's desk at work. No message on the answering machine at home. If Kate hadn't had that unexpected little heart-to-heart with Tucker in the hallway, she never would have known he'd conferred with Deirdre. Her friend hadn't kept her informed.

Finally Kate had been unable to stand it any longer. She'd reached for the phone. Deirdre was definitely defensive about her actions, another thing that took Kate by surprise.

"I should think you'd be applauding," Deirdre said now. "Weren't you the one who told me I should let the police handle this?"

Kate resisted the impulse to grind her teeth. "Yes," she replied.

"Some people might think I'd done you a favor," Deirdre went on. "Tucker was pretty clear about wanting you to butt out, as I recall."

"Your point being?"

"My point being, if he sees you're surprised by the fact that he and I have had a meeting, then he knows you're toeing the line," Deirdre proposed.

"Oh, that's just great," Kate said. "Kate Lockley, line-toeing wimp. Just the image I've spent years trying to foster. When you leave me out of the loop, you put me at a disadvantage. That's not a good position to be in with anybody, particularly a shark like Tucker."

"Look, Kate," Deirdre said. "It wasn't my intention to wrong-foot you with him, and if I did, I'm sorry. But I think I've been pretty clear about one thing from the start. I'm going to do whatever it takes to find out who killed my father. If Tucker suddenly decides I'm his new best friend, I'm his new best friend. End of story."

"Does Angel know?"

"I don't have any kind of exclusive arrangement with Angel," Deirdre said, irritation strong in her voice.

There was a pause.

"I'm sorry you're upset about this," Deirdre said after a moment. "But I really think you're making a mountain out of a molehill. All I did was give Tucker the information we tried to interest him in in the first place."

"I realize that," Kate said. "But next time I'd appreciate it if you'd keep me informed. I bent the rules for you, Dee. Frankly, I think that deserves a little more consideration."

"For Pete's sake, how many more times do you want me to say I'm sorry?"

There was another pause.

"Just promise me you won't go running to Angel," Deirdre said.

"No," Kate said evenly.

"What the hell do you mean, no?"

"I don't have to promise anything. You ought to know me well enough by now to know that I don't go running to anyone. You're Angel's client.

The way you handle yourself with him is your business, not mine. Good luck with your investigation, Deirdre. I'll see you around."

"Kate, wait," Deirdre protested.

Kate hit the Off button and cradled the receiver. As she shrugged into her shoulder harness in preparation for going back to work, the phone rang. Kate ignored it. She'd had about all the confrontations she cared to for today—a day which, for her, was actually just starting.

She slipped on her jacket, picked up her car keys, and headed for the door. The phone was still ringing as she left the apartment.

CHAPTER FOURTEEN

I shouldn't have been so hard on Doyle, Angel thought.

He was doing the best he could. The fact that his best and Angel's weren't the same thing was hardly Doyle's fault. Nor was the fact that, as far as Angel could tell, even his own best wasn't getting them very far.

I'll say I'm sorry, he decided. The next time he saw Doyle. He could only hope it wouldn't be the last time he'd see him, a distinct possibility, at the rate things were going.

Apparently, the demon's followers were upping the ante. Feutoch, or, as the press kept calling him, the Krispy Kritter Killer, had just struck two nights in a row.

Last night it had been a car fire that incinerated a kid in Beverly Hills. Tonight, an apartment fire in Westwood, which was where Angel was now. The demon had lucked out with this last bit of pyrotechnics. It had netted him a two-for-one.

From what Angel had been able to overhear on the street, the victims were Elise Madison, a waitress, and her live-in boyfriend, Stan McGraw. They'd been burned to death as they slept in their bed. As always, the fire had destroyed anything that might have showed evidence of a break-in. Or any evidence at all.

"I thought I might find you here," a voice said.

Surprised, Angel glanced down to find Deirdre Arensen by his side. Since their initial meeting, his only contact with Deirdre had been a phone call from her to say she hadn't turned up anything of interest in her recheck of her father's files. As Angel had had nothing new to report, either, the conversation had been short and not particularly sweet. Information, the thing they so desperately needed, being in short supply.

"What are you doing here?" Angel asked now.

Deirdre's eyebrows rose. She cocked her head in the direction of the apartment building and all the commotion in front of it.

"The same thing you are, I assume. Isn't it obvious?"

Angel grunted.

Deirdre folded her arms across her chest, her eyes still focused across the street. If she was offended by Angel's obvious lack of enthusiasm for her presence, she didn't show it.

"What's the current body count?"

"Fifteen," Angel answered.

"That we know about."

"That we know about."

"That makes three since Ellen Bradshaw."

Angel nodded.

"So, the pace is picking up."

"Looks that way," Angel said, his voice stony. "And for the record, you're not telling me anything I don't already know."

Deirdre glanced up. "So why don't you tell me something I don't know?" she proposed after a moment.

Angel met her eyes. "Such as?"

"What you're going to do about it."

Angel thrust his hands into his pockets. "I'm working on it."

"Work faster," Deirdre suggested, her tone sharp. "That's why I came to you, isn't it? Standing around at crime scenes is a thing I can do on my own. I thought you were supposed to be some kind of hotshot. Don't tell me you're already out of options."

"I didn't say that—" Angel started. He broke off as he spotted a fresh commotion across the street. The door of one of the police cruisers suddenly flew open, and the officer behind the wheel stuck his head out.

"Where's the Hick?" he yelled. "Somebody find Tucker. Get him over here. Now!"

"What the hell is it?" a second voice barked as a lean man in plainclothes materialized beside the patrol car. Everybody else backed up a step.

"That's Tucker," Deirdre murmured. "He's the guy in charge."

"Oh, yeah," Angel said. "The one everybody likes."

"This had better be good," Detective Tucker snarled. "I'm a little busy here, in case you hadn't noticed. And if I hear that nickname again, Stevenson, you're going to find yourself behind a desk pushing paper for the rest of your natural life."

By way of answer, Officer Stevenson held out the radio.

"Oh, shit," Angel said.

Deirdre glanced up, startled. "What?"

"There's been another one."

"Yes, Mama, of course I will wash my hands first. I know the money I handle is dirty. And I will eat this while it is warm."

As gently as he could, Rajit Singh escorted his mother to the door of the mini-mart where he worked the graveyard shift. He'd been trying to get her to stop bringing him a home-cooked meal for weeks now. It hardly enhanced the reputation he was trying to build, as a guy who could handle himself, when other people discovered his mother brought him his dinner.

But so far, no argument he'd advanced had worked. It was up to her to provide for him, she said. He was her one and only son.

"Call me when you get back to the apartment," Rajit instructed as he held the big glass door open for his mother. It was dangerous for a woman her age to be out so late at night, yet another argument that had gotten him nowhere. At least she always used the same cab company and often the same driver. Secretly Rajit suspected that she fed him, too.

He put his mother in the cab, then went back into the store and locked the door behind him. He wasn't supposed to do that. But he needed to use the head, which meant he'd be away from the register. He wasn't about to leave the store open.

Rajit went to the cash register, rang a No Sale, fished the weird coin he'd noticed when he came on out of the till, then shoved the cash drawer closed and made for the bathroom in the store's far corner. As he walked, he studied the coin. Perhaps it had some special value. It couldn't be put in with the regular deposit, that much was certain. Chances were good no one would even miss it. Rajit decided to have a smoke and think things over.

"Wait a minute," Deirdre Arensen sputtered. "What do you mean there's been another one? You can't know that. How can you know that?"

Angel jerked his head in the direction of the obviously agitated Tucker. "Your buddy over there just told me." He took Deirdre's elbow and propelled her along the sidewalk toward where he'd parked his car. "You were the one who wanted action," he said. "Come on. Let's go."

"Wait a minute," Deirdre said again, dragging her feet. "This could just be some wild-goose chase. I think we should stay here. We might be able to learn something. You don't know for sure that anything else has happened. You don't know where to go."

By way of answer, Angel stuffed her into the passenger seat, then leaned over to turn up the police radio. Tucker's strained and urgent voice filled the car.

"Oh, God," Deirdre Arensen whispered. "Oh, please, God, no."

Angel flipped open the glove compartment, yanked out a pad and pen, and thrust them into Deirdre's hands.

"When they provide a location, write it down."

Then he sprinted around to the driver's side, climbed in, put the key in the ignition, and gave it a vicious turn. The black Plymouth convertible roared to life. Over it, Angel could hear the dispatch operator's urgent voice. He looked at Deirdre, who was writing frantically.

"Where?"

"Culver City."

"Our boy gets around." Angel gunned the engine, put the car in gear, checked his rearview mirror, then shot out into the street. "Put your seat belt on."

Deirdre fastened her belt with a brisk click. "I'm not paying you to give me orders, you know."

"You haven't paid me at all, so far."

"Keep it up and the fee will stay the same. I can give you specific street directions as we get closer. Meantime, I suggest you shut up and drive."

Angel did that.

He drove fast, the top of the convertible down, letting the cool night air blow over him. Since leaving Westwood, Angel and Deirdre hadn't spoken. Angel had concentrated on driving down the 405. The only sound other than the rush of air, the whine of tires against the pavement, the whoosh of other cars moving past, had been the updates coming from the police radio.

Deirdre sat beside Angel, her dark hair tossing in the wind, her hands clutching the address of the Culver City fire in her lap. When she reached to brush her hair away from her face, Angel realized he'd felt the movement beside him several times before.

"Do you want me to put the top up?" he asked.

Deirdre shook her head. "No, don't. I like it,"

she said. "It feels . . . clean somehow. Like it's clearing the cobwebs from my brain."

"You are talking about the air in L.A., you realize."

Deirdre pulled her hair to one side and shot him a look. "I wondered how long it would take you to get over the sulks."

"I don't sulk," Angel replied. Sulking was a human luxury, one in which he hadn't indulged in more than two hundred years now. Brooding was more his style.

Deirdre released her hair so that it swarmed around her face again, obscuring her expression. "Okay. If you say so." She consulted the paper in her lap. "Not much farther now."

Angel changed lanes, moving to the right. He didn't want to miss the exit. To lose—waste—another second of time. It was already running out much faster than he liked.

"Something's happening, isn't it?" Deirdre suddenly said. "Something's wrong."

The police radio abruptly squawked to life. Angel listened for a moment, then, when it was clear it had nothing to do with the new fire, he reached to turn the radio down.

"What do you mean?" he asked. Though privately the same thing had been on his mind. The accelerated pace of the killings couldn't be good, not unless you were Feutoch or one of his followers.

"This two-in-the-same-night thing," Deirdre said. "That's never happened before, has it?"

"Not that we . . . ." Angel began.

". . . know of," Deirdre finished for him. She was silent for a moment, reaching to brush her hair back from her face as a sudden side gust of wind caught it and tossed it forward.

"I guess I was hoping we'd know more by now."

"You and me both," Angel told her. He moved over another lane. "Of course, this could be what's supposed to happen, when Feutoch gets close to his actual head count. Maybe this is normal."

"No."

Surprised by the vehemence in Deirdre's tone, Angel took his eyes off the road briefly to glance over at her. "How do you know?"

Deirdre colored. "I don't. Not for sure. It's just this impression I have from my father's notes. The deaths happen at a certain pace for a reason."

"Do your father's notes say why?"

Deirdre shook her head. "If they had, I'd have told you. If I had to guess, I'd say it's some sort of built-in safety device, probably left over from the early days of the cult. Frighten the local population too much, too soon . . ."

"They panic, start looking for scapegoats, and you run the risk of the cult being wiped out."

"It is a good point."

"A very good one."

"But it still leaves us with the same question, doesn't it?" Deirdre asked. "Why increase the pace now?"

Angel concentrated on driving for a moment. "Maybe somebody's decided to stop playing by the rules," he said.

In which case, his save-the-world effort could be in even worse shape than he'd thought. How close to manifesting all the time was Feutoch? Angel still didn't know. All he knew for sure was that the demon hadn't gotten there yet. If he had, the freeway Angel was speeding down would be one big ball of fire by now.

"Why do you suppose they do it?" Deirdre asked suddenly. "Feutoch's followers?"

Angel shot her another quick glance, this time of surprise. "I should have thought that would be obvious. He can make their dreams come true. Give them anything they want."

"Yes, but"—Deirdre shifted position, turning toward him—"how on earth do they live with themselves? How do you walk around knowing that the only reason you have the life you do is because you were willing to kill someone?"

The same way everybody else does, Angel thought. One step at a time.

"They don't actually have to do the killing themselves," he said aloud. "That makes it a whole lot easier to convince yourself it doesn't have anything to do with you. It's just another random event, an accident, and accidents happen all the time."

"But these aren't accidents," Deirdre insisted.

"You don't have to tell me," Angel said. "But you asked why. I'm telling you the way I think it works. Not having to get their hands messy lets people off the hook. Lets them tell themselves they're not responsible. Whoever set this up in the first place definitely understood the human psyche."

"Why doesn't that make me feel any better?"

"Probably because it's not supposed to," Angel said shortly. "But, hey—look on the bright side. Maybe they don't all do so well. Maybe more than we think end up like Ellen Bradshaw."

"Wanting out, you mean?" Deirdre asked.

Angel nodded. "Since we don't know who Feutoch's followers are, we have no way of knowing how many of them also become his victims. What we do know is, once you sign up, the demon's got you right where he wants you."

"Live with yourself or don't live at all?"

"Catchy motto. Either way, Feutoch adds to his head count."

"So, you're saying we can't win?" Deirdre asked.

"No," Angel answered. It wasn't that they couldn't win. It was just that, with the exception of their lone ace in the form of Terri Miller, the demon held all the really good cards.

"This is it," Deirdre said suddenly. "Take this exit, then go right at the stop sign." Angel hit his turn signal, preparing to get off. "After that you—" Deirdre began.

"I think I can manage it," Angel interrupted. All he'd have to do was follow the sound of the sirens.

"I hate this," Deirdre choked out several moments later. "This is awful. I want it to stop."

On the far side of her a man gave a harsh laugh. "Take a number and get in line."

Deirdre and Angel were part of a crowd across the street from a convenience store. Deirdre's presence, to say nothing of a swarm of cops, was forcing Angel to keep his distance, when he would have liked to be a whole lot closer. Details were trickling through, though. The moments when Angel appreciated rapacious television reporters were few and far between, but it looked as if tonight would be one of them.

The victim was the store clerk, Rajit Singh. He'd been incinerated in the convenience store bathroom. Police were still trying to calm his hysterical mother, who'd been pulling out of the store parking lot in a cab when the incident had occurred. She'd brought her son a home-cooked

193

meal right around midnight, the way she always did when he worked graveyard.

According to Mrs. Singh, her son had walked her to the cab, then locked the store's glass doors behind him and gone to wash his hands before eating the dinner she'd brought. That was the routine he always followed, she said. Her son was a good boy. She'd raised him to be clean.

The big glass doors of the convenience store had still been locked when the police arrived. They'd had to smash through them to get in. The fact that the sprinkler system had come on automatically had confined the fire damage to the bathroom. But the rest of the store was soaked.

And the locked door did tend to indicate that Rajit Singh had believed himself to be alone in the store when he'd been killed.

"Who the hell is this guy?" the man who'd spoken to Deirdre earlier suddenly exclaimed aloud. "Some kind of Harry Houdini?"

There was a flurry of activity across the street. Two uniformed officers were carrying a stretcher. On it, or so Angel assumed, was all that remained of Rajit Singh. His mother was trying to throw herself across the stretcher. The police restrained her. As Angel and Deirdre watched, a policewoman came forward, took Mrs. Singh by the shoulders, and gently yet firmly led her away. They made it half a dozen steps before Mrs. Singh collapsed onto the glass-strewn sidewalk, sobbing.

Deirdre turned to Angel, her expression fierce. "I want to go," she said. "Get me out of here."

"Sorry about that," Deirdre said several moments later. She took a sip of coffee, grimacing at the taste. "This is even worse than the stuff you serve."

"Oh, good, you're insulting me. Now I know you're feeling better," Angel said.

They were sitting in all-night coffee shop. Angel had decided to take a time-out before heading back to Westwood. Deirdre's car was still parked near the apartment building where Feutoch's earlier two victims du jour had met their ends.

"No, really, I mean it," Deirdre said.

"I don't make that coffee myself, you know."

"About being sorry," Deirdre said. "I just didn't expect it to hit me like that—the whole parent-child thing. There was just something about seeing that boy's mother . . ." Her voice trailed off.

"That's okay," Angel said. He didn't bother to say he understood, because he didn't. Even when he'd been human, his relationship with his parents hadn't been the best.

Deirdre took a second sip of coffee, not seeming to notice the taste this time. She set the mug back down on the table, then met Angel's eyes.

"We're going to lose, aren't we?" she asked.

"No, we're not."

"How can you say that? Three new deaths

tonight alone. And we're no better than the police. We've got nothing to go on."

"That's not true," Angel said. "We know what we're really up against."

Deirdre gave a snort. "Pardon me if that information doesn't impel me to do handstands in the aisle. Ignorance just might be bliss here, Angel."

"Ignorance is never bliss," Angel said. "And you're forgetting Terri Miller."

"Who the hell is Terri Miller?"

"Cordelia's next-door neighbor," Angel said. "You remember, the one who—"

"I remember," Deirdre snapped. "What about her?"

"She and Doyle went out. They established a rapport."

"Doyle!" Deirdre exploded. She lowered her voice as heads turned in their direction. "You gave something as important as this to Doyle?"

"Doyle has hidden depths," Angel answered. A thing he'd chosen to overlook not long ago. "Besides, it turns out he knew her from before. Not well, but enough to have established a connection. I thought it best for him to do the follow-up."

"So they went out and . . ."

"And she won't go out with him tonight."

"I knew it!" Deirdre exploded. "I told you so. She's our only real lead, and now he's blown it."

"She won't go out with him," Angel continued, riding right over her, "because she has to go to a meeting of some kind. One she said she *couldn't get out of.*"

Deirdre shut her mouth with a snap. "Oh."

In the silence that followed, Angel took a sip of water. It wasn't that he was thirsty, but the action helped him look normal.

"You think it's a cult meeting?" Deirdre asked.

"I think it's possible."

"How will you find out?"

"Doyle's going to follow her."

"And what are you going to do?"

"I'm going to follow Doyle."

A slow smile began to spread across Deirdre Arensen's face. "Don't forget to take along your bread crumbs."

"Thanks for the reminder," Angel said. "I knew there was another stop I needed to make on the way home."

He was in the bar when his pager went off. A sudden agitation from inside his suit coat pocket. On the same side as his heart, though it might be considered an assumption to say that he still had one. Working at Wolfram and Hart could do strange things to one's insides.

He took the beeper out, checked the number, took a last swallow of beer, and threw a couple of bills down on the bar. If he noticed the regret in the blond bartender's eyes as he slid from his stool and headed for the exit, he didn't let it show.

He waited until he was inside his car before punching the number into his cell. The phone was answered on the first ring.

"I got your page."

He listened intently to the voice on the other end.

"Yes, thank you, I do find that very interesting," he commented. "Is there anything more?"

Again, he listened, more briefly this time. "I understand," he said. "I'll make sure it's taken care of. Yes, I do realize that."

He hit the Off button, snapped the phone shut, and tossed it into the glove compartment. Then he sat for a moment, fingering some unseen object in his pocket. He pulled it out, flipping it into the air in a quick coin toss.

"Heads, you lose; tails, you lose," he murmured.

It was the Mark of Feutoch.

CHAPTER FIFTEEN

"I still think you should have told Doyle."

"I heard you the first time, Cordelia," Angel said. "The answer is still the same. No."

He was sitting in the car, top up, in the parking garage of Cordelia's apartment. It had taken most of the day, but Angel had finally convinced himself to let Cordy in on his plan to shadow Terri and Doyle. He didn't like it much, but in the end he'd been forced to admit he didn't have a choice. He needed her help. The first part of the evening's festivities would take place before the sun went down.

Adept as Angel was at finding ways to protect himself from acquiring a fatal sunburn, when he added the need to watch Doyle without Doyle being aware of it to the equation, he didn't much like the way the math turned out. Too many ways to get spotted, or worse.

Which explained why he was lying flat on his back in the front seat of his car, top up, talking to Cordelia on his cell phone from the apartment building's parking garage.

"You're doing just what they want you to," Cordelia's voice came through the phone. "You know—all for one . . ." As she realized the quote wasn't going to go quite the way she wanted, her voice faltered and broke off.

"I think you mean divide and conquer," Angel said. "But the answer's still the same, Cord."

"Sheesh," Cordy said. "Who gave you a stubborn pill this morning?"

"Look, I told you, it's better this way," Angel said. "Safer for Doyle. If he doesn't know I'm there, he can't accidentally tip anybody else off."

"He wouldn't do that," Cordelia protested.

"Not on purpose," Angel agreed. "Which would explain my use of the term *accidentally.*"

"I know what *accidentally* means, Angel," Cordelia said, her tone waspish. "You don't have to get all S.A.T. on me. I did graduate, you know. Okay, hold on. I think something's happening."

There was a pause. Angel eased his keys out of his pocket and slipped them into the ignition.

"She's leaving the apartment," Cordelia's voice confirmed.

"Which direction is she going?"

"Not toward the garage," Cord said after a moment. "I think she's going to walk."

"Where's Doyle? Can you see him? Has he got her?"

"Not yet—okay, he's got her," Cordelia said. "Pull out of the garage and turn right."

Angel sat up, switched on the ignition. "Thanks, Cordelia."

"Oh, hey—anytime you want someone to spy on a co-worker, you know who to call."

The cell went dead as Cordelia severed the connection. Slowly Angel nosed the Plymouth out of the parking garage.

Inside her apartment Cordelia hung up the phone in disgust. She'd done things during her years as the reigning bitch of Sunnydale High she wasn't proud of now, but nothing that had made her feel quite so slimy as the thing she'd just done. The thing Angel had asked her to do. Spy on Doyle. It didn't even help that she could, in fact, see Angel's point.

If Doyle concentrated on Terri, that left Angel free to concentrate on . . . whatever else there was to concentrate on. And if Doyle didn't know Angel was there, nothing in his behavior could tip the whatever else off. But something about the setup still didn't sit right with Cordelia. They were a team. They ought to function as one.

Restlessly she prowled around her apartment, then moved back to the window, staring out. People didn't walk together anymore, she'd noticed.

As much as possible in a place as crowded as L.A., they walked alone. She'd even seen people cross the street to avoid coming too close. And it wasn't just strangers people were afraid of. The newspaper accounts of the recent deaths, particularly the couple toasted as they slept in their own bed, had brought new meaning to that catchy phrase *trust no one*.

The Krispy Kritter Killer could be anyone, the papers claimed. Even someone you knew and loved.

Not likely, Cordelia thought. But then, the people who wrote the papers didn't know the truth. Didn't know the Krispy Kritter was actually a fire demon named Feutoch. A thing probably only a mother fire demon could love.

On impulse Cordy turned around, her back to the window, and surveyed her apartment, as if for the first time. It was a great place, and she genuinely appreciated living here, particularly compared to where she'd lived before. She liked it so much, she was even willing to put up with a resident ghost for a roommate.

But would she have killed to live here? Targeted somebody else to die? Cordy herself would have been the first to admit she wasn't particularly given to introspection. Or caring for those she didn't know. But still, she didn't think so. The old Cordelia Chase, maybe. On a really self-absorbed day. But not the person she was now.

And it was largely due to Angel, she realized suddenly.

Angel, who had one hundred plus years' worth of things Cordelia didn't even want to imagine to make up for. Who was the living embodiment of what it meant not to leave one's past behind, but to carry it with you, always. A burden you could never set down. Until some outside agency decided you'd done enough. You'd atoned.

Assuming that Angel could actually be considered the living embodiment of anything, of course.

Did the fact that he was officially dead mean that Angel couldn't dream? Cordelia wondered all of a sudden. She knew that he could love. She'd seen the truly disastrous results. One instant of happiness and blammo. You went back to being a soulless demon, and all your good intentions literally went straight to hell.

If Angel could take Feutoch's bargain, what would he wish for? To be human again? To start over? Or would he wish to simply lay down all the burdens he carried and let the end of the world come? Was that what all this sneaking around behind Doyle's back was really about? And wasn't that an exceptionally not-so-pretty thought?

Cordelia heard a sound from the kitchen. The *whoosh* of the refrigerator door as it opened, then closed. As she watched, a cold can of soda drifted through the kitchen doorway on its way straight toward her.

"Whoa," Cordelia said. "That bad, huh?" The can hovered in midair. Cordelia reached for it, popped the top, and took a swallow. "Thanks, Dennis. I guess I needed that."

A girl knew things were getting out of hand when even a ghost could tell she was thinking way too much.

"So," she said, "how far away do you think he is, by now? I mean, I couldn't possibly find him, right? He's got way too much of a head start."

Silence filled the apartment. Then to Cordy's astonishment, a set of keys rose and hovered in the air. A tiny stuffed bear dangled from the end of the keychain.

"Omigod. You stole me a car."

I must be losing it, Terri thought.

It was the only explanation she could come up with for the feeling that had come over her not long after she'd left her apartment. The sense that she was being followed. She told herself that she was being foolish. It wasn't midnight in some alley on a dark and stormy night. It was a lovely spring evening in L.A.

Besides, who on earth would want to follow her? One of the Illuminati? But that didn't make sense at all. Her second thoughts were long over, had been ever since she'd gone out with Doyle.

She detoured around a man in a well-cut business suit who'd stopped to talk on his cell phone.

His eyes slid to hers, then jerked away. They were bloodshot. *I'm probably just picking up on L.A.'s overall paranoia,* she thought.

Terri paused and fumbled in her purse for the slip of paper with the address of tonight's meeting written on it. She didn't know who'd sent it. It had simply arrived in her mailbox yesterday morning. But she'd figured it was Andy. He was the one who'd found her the apartment, after all.

It would be good to see Andy again, Terri decided. She wanted him to know how well she was doing, how quickly she'd settled into the life she'd chosen. She might even tell him about Doyle. Not by name, just casually let slip the fact that she was seeing someone.

The address on the slip of paper was about half a block around the next corner, Terri decided. She stuffed the piece of paper back inside her purse, and picked up the pace.

"Terri!" a familiar voice exclaimed. "There you are!"

She knows, Doyle thought.

Terri hadn't turned around, but there was something about the way she held her body, the tense set of her shoulders, that told him she suspected she was being watched. It only went to confirm the thing he'd been thinking ever since he'd started his vigil outside her apartment.

He couldn't afford to blow things this time.

The trouble was, following somebody was a lot harder than it looked, particularly in what was essentially broad daylight. Doyle didn't come equipped with any of the little perks film P.I.s always seemed to have. Long shadows to lurk in. Convenient shop windows to stop and peer into. Clever disguises to don at a moment's notice. He came equipped as . . . Doyle.

The fact that he had a disguise that could top any film P.I.'s in twenty seconds flat didn't help much. He hardly thought the best way to remain inconspicuous was to put his demon face on.

Terri halted on the sidewalk, rooted in her purse, and pulled out a piece of paper. Doyle skidded to a stop so suddenly the guy several steps behind him almost mowed him down. Ordinarily a situation like that might have provoked a confrontation. Instead, the guy sidestepped swiftly, then scurried on by, head down, his eyes carefully avoiding Doyle's.

Nobody wanted to do anything that might make an impression, Doyle thought. Impressions made you memorable. If you could be remembered, you could be turned into a target. And targets could be brought down.

Doyle held his position, body turned away, face angled over his left shoulder toward Terri. *Come on*, he thought. *Take me where I want to go. Help me. Help us all*.

He continued to hold as Terri stuck the paper

back into her purse and started to walk once more. She was just a few steps away from a corner. Which way would she go? Doyle waited until Terri had swung to the right and disappeared from view before he sprinted after her. He couldn't afford to lose her now.

Well, at least there was one thing in his favor, Angel thought, as he pulled to a stop at a red light. Doyle and Terri, or, to put them in their proper order, Terri and Doyle, hadn't exactly been moving at breakneck speed. Hence Angel's being more than happy to stop at a red light.

The sun had finally gone down. It would be light for quite a while yet, but the big bad orb of day had actually slipped down over the edge of the horizon. That meant it was safe for Angel to move around. Now, if Doyle and Terri would only get where they were going so he could actually *do* something.

The light changed and Angel accelerated through the intersection, pulling the car to the curb about a block behind where Doyle had stopped, abruptly.

What's the holdup? Angel wondered.

He could feel the tension in his arms as he gripped the steering wheel. It was hours yet, till midnight. But ever since the Mark of Feutoch had tumbled from Cordelia's bag, Angel had had a permanent countdown in the back of his brain.

Every second that ticked by brought him closer to the very real possibility of Deirdre Arensen's death, to say nothing of countless others.

Unfortunately, it didn't seem to bringing him closer to the thing he needed to know.

What he had to do to stop it.

He sat up a little straighter as he saw Doyle move forward. To the next corner, then around it. *Finally!* Angel glanced in the rearview mirror, then pulled out into traffic, moving slowly.

"Terri, there you are!"

At the sound of Andy's voice, Terri skidded to a stop. She'd been so intent on locating the right building she hadn't noticed him, standing under the covered entry to the high-rise.

"Andy," she said. "Hi."

"You're almost late," Andy said, his blue eyes searching hers swiftly. "I was afraid you weren't coming."

"Oh," Terri said. "No—I mean—I'm sorry. Of course I was coming. I didn't mean to be late."

"So," Andy said. "How's it going?"

Terri began to worry the strap of her purse. Why did she feel so nervous, like he was giving her the third degree all of a sudden? She hadn't done anything wrong. If anything, she'd done just what they'd told her to. *Pull yourself together, Miller.*

"Fine. I did what I was supposed to. I passed on the—"

"Hey," Andy broke in, his tone joking. "Slow down. This isn't a test. I just wanted to know how you were doing, that's all. Some people find the transition kind of tough. That's why we encourage new members to come to a follow-up meeting right off."

"Of course," Terri said. *Idiot,* she told herself. "I'm happy, Andy. Honestly, I am."

"I'm glad to hear that," Andy said with a smile. "I tell you what, after the meeting, why don't you let me walk you home? You can tell me all about how it's going. Give me all the details."

"Okay," Terri said. She'd wait till then to tell him about Doyle, she thought.

"Ready to go in?" Andy asked. He took a step forward as if to take her arm. As he did so, Terri caught a flash of movement out of the corner of her eye. She turned toward it, gave a start of surprise.

"Doyle?"

CHAPTER SIXTEEN

Well, shit, Doyle thought.

He'd been caught, and he'd no one but himself to blame. He'd been stupid, that's what it was. By the time he'd reached the corner, Terri was out of sight. In response, he'd done the thing only the lamest film P.I.s did. He'd started to run. It was the sudden slamming on of the brakes when he'd finally spotted her that had attracted Terri's attention.

So much for not blowing things this time around.

He made a swift survey of the building's entry, noted the guy standing next to Terri. For the first time, Doyle felt a stab of doubt. Had he gotten it wrong after all? Had Terri turned him down tonight because she had a date with another guy?

In the next moment he'd plastered his best impression of a golden retriever on his face. You learned so much more when other people thought you were friendly but not too bright.

"Terri," he said. "Hi."

"Doyle, what are you doing here?" Terri asked, her voice slightly dazed.

"Oh, nothin' special. You know, just walking by. Then I spotted you and—" Doyle let his voice fade away, as if he'd run out of explanations. Which he had. "So," he continued brightly after a moment. "This where your meeting is, or what?"

"My meeting," Terri echoed.

"Terri," the other guy spoke up for the first time. "Why don't you introduce me to your friend?"

"Oh, um," Terri said. "Andy, this is Doyle."

"Pleased to meetcha," Doyle said, extending his hand, his expression affable, even though he hated the other guy on sight. Andy had the kind of blond-haired, blue-eyed L.A. looks Doyle despised. On a guy.

"Likewise," Andy said. They shook on it. "So, how do you guys know each other?" he inquired. His tone was mild, but Doyle could see the watchful look in the back of his eyes.

"Chance," he said. "Totally. I work with Terri's next-door neighbor. We all got acquainted while Terri was moving in."

"That's a nice coincidence," Andy said.

Doyle beamed at him. "I thought so." There was a quick, strained silence. "Well," Doyle went on. "I guess I should be motoring. I know you guys have . . . things . . . to do. But we're still on for tomorrow, Terri, right?"

No sense in letting Mr. Tall, Blond, and Handsome think he could have things all his way.

"Right," Terri said. Her head swiveled back and forth between him and Andy, as if she could sense the strange undercurrents but couldn't figure out why they were there, Doyle thought.

"We're not doing anything special," Andy suddenly put in. "Just a get-together with some people with mutual interests. Why don't you come along?"

"I wouldn't want to gate-crash," Doyle said.

"Don't be ridiculous," Andy protested. "We'd love it if you'd join us, wouldn't we, Terri?" He slipped a possessive hand beneath one of her elbows.

Terri's eyes had gone wide and startled, the irises so huge she looked as if she were straining to see in a room that had suddenly been plunged into the dark.

"Sure," she managed. "If you say so, Andy."

"That settles it, then," Andy said. He smiled at Doyle, a row of perfect white teeth, and gestured toward the entrance to the building. "Shall we?"

I sure as hell hope Doyle knows what he's doing, Angel thought.

He'd found a parking place quickly, miracle of

miracles, even though he'd had to squash down a quick spurt of guilt for having beaten an old lady driving a turquoise blue Fairlane to the spot. She'd honked and shaken her fist at him as he'd gotten out of the Plymouth. That had helped to ease his guilt. A lot. That and the knowledge that, if he didn't relocate Doyle quickly, nobody was going to have to worry about finding a place to park anymore.

Angel sprinted the couple of blocks back to Doyle's last location. He was just in time to see him enter a tall apartment building, right behind a woman Angel assumed was Terri Miller. Angel could see the outline of a guy inside, holding the door.

He waited until the maw of the apartment building had swallowed Doyle before he moved.

Doyle had gone in his way. So far, so good. But Angel had ways of his own.

This is stupid, Cordelia thought. She must be out of her mind.

It was ridiculous to feel this impulse to follow Angel, as if he might need her. As if he couldn't take care of himself. Neither thing was true, and nobody knew it better than Cordy herself. So why wasn't she at home, watching TV while she did her nails? Why was she out driving around in a . . . borrowed car. A Lexus that had turned out to belong to Terri Miller. Apparently, the furnishings of her apartment had included a brand-new car.

Totally irritated with herself, with the whole situation, Cordy hit her turn signal and randomly turned right. She *was* out of her mind. How did she expect to find Angel when she didn't even know which direction he'd gone? Her behavior, to say nothing of Dennis's, was totally out of character, and it was all Angel's fault. If he hadn't insisted on following Doyle without Doyle knowing about it . . .

Wrong. Wrong. Wrong, Cordelia thought. Why couldn't Angel just see that—

With a squeal of tires, Cordelia hit the brakes and skidded to a stop. The car ahead of her, an ancient turquoise blue Ford Fairlane, had jerked to the right and slammed to a halt, completely blocking a parked car. A black Plymouth convertible with the top down.

That's Angel's car.

Cordelia hit the accelerator, whipped around the Fairlane and into a parking space that had just become available near the corner. As she got out of the car, she saw the white-haired driver of the Fairlane remove an umbrella from the trunk and begin to jab at the tires of Angel's car.

I don't even want to know, Cordelia decided. What she wanted was to find Angel. Now.

Septimus was exhausted. He'd walked so long, he'd lost all sense of time. He was hungry. He couldn't remember when he'd last eaten, but he thought it had been *that* night, the night of the fire.

He didn't know at what point he'd realized the truth: He was being punished. He'd taken the envelope, the one with the pretty stamps. He shouldn't have done it. It had been bad. And bad acts would always be punished. His only hope of finding Terri lay in giving up the thing he'd wanted so to show her in the first place.

He had to give the envelope back. He had to make a sacrifice.

He didn't want to do it. Over the days he'd carried it, the envelope had only grown more precious to him. But he knew he didn't have a choice. Septimus knew the way the world worked. You got nothing for nothing.

He was sobbing by the time he found a mailbox. Pulled the handle down, placed the envelope reverently into the opening, then released the handle suddenly so that the door closed with a hollow booming sound. It seemed to reverberate inside Septimus's aching head. Pressing his hands against it, he staggered away, not noticing the way people on the sidewalk scattered before him.

Please, he thought. *Just let me find her. Just let the nightmare be over.*

The way Doyle had it figured, either he was in or he was in big trouble.

He stood in the elevator, Terri between him and the guy called Andy. He could feel the air filled with tension, wondered if it was his own, or somebody else's. He probably ought to be making snappy conversation. Too bad he couldn't think of any.

The elevator rose swiftly, stopped at the designated floor. It pinged once, and the doors slid open. Thirteenth floor, Doyle noted. Not surprising. Andy moved first, escorting Terri out, one hand still wrapped possessively around her elbow. Doyle followed as they moved off down the hall. All of a sudden Andy stopped.

"You go on ahead," he told Terri as he released the hold on her arm. "Last door on the right."

Terri's startled eyes shot to Doyle, then away. "Oh, but . . ." she faltered.

Andy flashed her a smile that didn't quite reach his eyes. "Do as I ask, please, Terri," he said. "I need to make sure Doyle understands what this is all about. Don't you think he deserves a little background? You got some."

"Okay, Andy," Terri said, though her uncertainty was plain. "If you say so."

"Tell you what," Doyle broke in. "Andy can fill me in, then I'll catch up with you. How about you save me a seat?"

Terri licked her lips. "Okay," she said again. She turned and walked to the end of the hall.

"Don't bother to knock. Just go on in," Andy called.

Terri did as he instructed. The *click* of the door as it closed behind her was loud in the corridor.

"So, what is this stuff I need to know?" Doyle asked as Andy turned toward him.

"This."

Doyle felt the air shoot from his lungs as Andy's fist rammed into his stomach. Wheezing in pain and surprise, Doyle doubled over. Andy followed with a hard right that had Doyle spinning around, his head snapping back to connect with the wall with a sound like ripe watermelons splitting open. Stars wheeled before his face. He never even saw the third blow coming. It dropped him like a stone.

Andy kicked him once, twice, as if for good measure. Then he crouched down. "Let me give you some advice, my new friend Doyle. If you want to stay alive, stay away from Terri Miller. Where she goes, what she does, is my business, not yours."

He stood. Through the roaring that filled his head, Doyle heard Andy's footsteps move off down the hall.

Inside the meeting room Terri jerked to attention as Andy came to stand behind her chair.

"Did it go all right?" she asked, twisting her head around in an attempt to see his face. "Where's Doyle?"

Andy shot his shirt cuffs, then nodded his head

in the direction of the two men standing on either side of the door. They were the same ones that had dealt with Joy Clement, Terri realized suddenly. Not until they'd left the room did Andy glance down at her, his expression cold.

"Let's just say he changed his mind."

What he wanted, Angel thought, was some good old-fashioned darkness. Preferably of the Stygian kind. The type of darkness that treated you like a lover, wrapped you in its arms. Encouraged secret deeds, then made them possible.

What did he have instead? Almost bright-as-day Southern California twilight. It was enough to make a guy look for a new line of work, assuming the guy in question had that option. Angel didn't, which explained why he was loitering in the parking area behind the apartment building he'd seen Doyle and Terri enter. The setup looked pretty standard, he thought.

An elevator that would most likely open if he pushed the button but wouldn't take him anywhere unless he had an access code. That left him with a couple of choices. He could wait until he spotted a tenant, then hitch a ride. A thing that could take who knows how long when he didn't have any time to waste.

Or he could look for less orthodox options.

Angel was just deciding on the second approach when he heard a sound behind him. The scrape of a hard-soled shoe against the concrete flooring of the parking garage. Senses going on full alert, Angel began to turn, resisting the impulse to swing around abruptly. There was no sense frightening the person who might be his ticket inside.

A car. I didn't hear a car, he thought. He completed the turn in one fluid motion. Standing in front of him, form outlined by the light behind him, was a guy. In his right hand he held a gun, the barrel pointed straight at Angel's chest. Angel threw himself to the right just as his unknown adversary fired.

It missed his heart.

Angel felt the projectile catch him in the shoulder, slamming him back against the elevator doors. They parted, and he stumbled back, his knees giving way beneath him. He fell to the elevator floor.

The guy advanced, firing again, into the exposed skin of Angel's neck this time. Angel could feel the sharp tip of the projectile burn as it pierced his skin.

Not a bullet, he thought.

He tried to push himself upright. Found he couldn't do it. The lower half of his body seemed to have lost the ability to function. The only way he knew it was still there was because he could still see it. He couldn't feel his legs at all.

Angel groped at his neck, came away with a

tiny dart that looked like it belonged on *Croco-dile Hunter. Tranquilizer dart,* he thought. Either that, or some incredibly fast-acting poison. Either way, he'd been bagged like a water buffalo.

Angel lay on the floor of the elevator staring upward as his unknown adversary came to stand over him.

"Who—" he managed to get out.

The guy smiled. Angel really hated it when they did that. Particularly when they looked like they'd stepped off the cover of *GQ.*

"My name isn't important. What *is* important is that I'm an emissary from your friends at Wolfram and Hart."

Angel's tongue felt thick and rubbery. It was an effort to get it to function.

"I've got a news flash for you," he said. "I don't have any friends at Wolfram and Hart."

The man's smile got a little wider. "You got that right. The partners would like all that to change, though. They asked me to deliver this token of their esteem."

He knelt by Angel's side, reached into his own suit coat pocket, removed an object. He held it up in front of Angel's face.

It was the Mark of Feutoch.

"I don't suppose I need to tell you what this is."

Angel made an indeterminate sound.

"I didn't think so," Mr. *GQ* said. He flipped the coin over, revealing the side with the ring of fire.

Inside the ring was the number one. "You know what the number means, I assume?"

This time Angel managed a growl.

"Midnight tomorrow you're toast, Angelus. Unless, of course, you get yourself off the hook before then by passing on the Mark. But you won't do that, will you? Not now that you've gone all Goody Two-shoes. Mr. Get Involved with the Poor, Innocent Mortals. We're not all so innocent, you know."

He opened Angel's trenchcoat, tucked the Mark of Feutoch into the inside breast pocket. Then he closed the trenchcoat, buttoned the top button, gave Angel's chest a friendly little pat.

"Just a little more than twenty-four hours from now, our problems will be at an end, and so will yours. And there's not a damn thing you can do to stop it." He smiled at Angel sweetly. "Unless, of course, you'd care to sell that soul of yours."

The guy rose, dusting off his pantlegs as he did so, and stepped back out of the elevator.

"Glad we could have this little chat," he said. "Somehow, I don't think I'll see you around."

Angel was still trying to get his tongue to frame a suitable response when the elevator doors slid shut and the elevator began to rise.

Cordelia scanned the street anxiously. Which way, into which building, had Doyle and Angel gone? The truth was, there was absolutely no way to tell. Which meant she'd have to try them all.

And look for what, exactly? she thought. Somehow, she didn't think she could just march right up to any of these apartment buildings, scan the list of tenants for the one named Feutoch. Cordelia made a sound of frustration. This was what she got for letting a ghost talk her into something. *Come on, you can do this,* she told herself. *Pull a Willow. Reason it out.*

Doyle was following Terri. Angel was following Doyle. That meant Doyle would have gone wherever Terri did. Like say, for instance, through the front door. But Angel would be much less likely to take the head-on approach. He'd reconnoiter. Look for another way in. Preferably one that wasn't so high profile.

The back door. *That's it,* Cordelia thought. If she wanted to find Angel, that's where she had to go.

Septimus didn't want to walk anymore. His legs were acting funny, refusing to hold him up. If he kept moving, he was afraid that he'd fall down. He knew what happened then. Somebody would call the cops. They'd put him in a cell. He might get a meal that way, but it wouldn't be worth it. Septimus couldn't stand being locked up. Couldn't bear to be confined. He'd had enough of that when he was young. The first thing he'd promised himself when he'd left home was that nobody was ever going to lock him inside of anything ever again.

All he needed was someplace quiet, a place with a dark corner where he could lie down. Maybe one of those undercover places where people parked their cars. Sometimes he even found money on the ground in places like that. Change fallen from a pocket. Now and then a stray dollar. If that happened, he could get himself something to eat, after he'd rested. After it really got dark.

He'd done the right thing. He'd put the envelope back where it belonged. Surely his luck was going to change for the better.

There. That was the place, he thought. About halfway down the block. He'd seen a guy in a fancy suit come out on foot, but no cars going in or out. It would be quiet there. It would be safe. For a while. Running one arm along the back of the building for support, Septimus made his way toward the parking garage.

Angel had a bad feeling about his current situation. He thought it had to do with the fact that he was pretty much a sitting duck. He didn't think the errand boy from Wolfram and Hart had sent the elevator on its sudden journey. But that was hardly the same thing as saying this trip was innocent, or that it would turn out all right.

From his position on his back, Angel watched as the floor numbers illuminated briefly, then winked out, one by one. When it reached the thirteenth floor, it stopped.

Perfect, Angel thought. He did his best to prop himself up against the back wall of the elevator. If he was going to have to face something, he'd rather do it sitting up.

He watched as the elevator doors slid open. Three guys stood in the hall. Actually, it was two guys standing and one guy being supported between them. A guy who had plainly just taken something of a beating.

A guy who looked a lot like Doyle.

"I had no idea this was such a tough neighborhood, did you?" the guy on the right asked as he caught sight of Angel.

The guy on the left shook his head. "No idea at all."

"Who do you guys think you are?" Angel got out, pleased to discover his tongue was working better. Now, if only he could get his legs to do the same. "Tweedledum and Tweedledee?"

"Hey—a comedian," the tough guy on the left, Tweedledum, said.

"Yeah," Tweedledee put in. "Too bad he's not a stand-up." He snickered at his own lame joke. "So, funny boy," he went on. "How'd you like a captive audience?"

Together, the two toughs heaved Doyle across

Angel's still-useless legs. He could hear their laughter as the doors slid closed and the elevator began its journey back down.

It was seeing the street person that made Cordelia decide which building to investigate first. There were lots of homeless in L.A., but you didn't often see one in this part of town. But there he was, a guy in a too-large camouflage coat, moving down the alley. In spite of the fact that he looked more than a little unsteady on his feet, he moved with purpose, as if he knew exactly where he was going.

Why is that? Cordelia wondered. Had he seen something she hadn't gotten there in time to see? She lingered at the corner of the alley, waiting until the guy disappeared into a parking garage. Then she sprinted after him, the keys clenched through the fingers of her right hand. There was no sense in taking too many chances, after all.

Cordy slowed her pace as she neared the garage. Her ears straining, listening for the slightest sound. She could have sworn she heard a *ping,* like the sound an elevator makes when it's arrived at its destination. A moment later, voices.

That's Angel! she thought.

Quick as lightning, Cordelia ducked around the corner and into the parking garage. She was just in time to see the guy in the camouflage coat bending over something in the elevator.

"Hey!" she shouted.

The guy in the coat straightened so abruptly he almost lost his balance. He held up his hands, as if Cordelia had announced he was under arrest, then rushed past her, out of the parking garage. Cordelia hurried to the elevator.

Doyle and Angel were both inside. Angel was trying to get to his feet. Doyle was out cold.

"Looks like you found him," Cordelia remarked.

"Let's do the sarcasm later, shall we?" Angel suggested. "Right now I'd really like to get out of this elevator and back to the office. Since you scared off my friend there, maybe you'd be willing to lend a shoulder."

"Fine. Right. Don't bother to thank me," Cordelia grumbled as she complied.

"How'd you know where to find me, anyway?" Angel asked, when they'd succeeded in getting Doyle to his feet.

"I followed you," she said shortly. "How else?"

CHAPTER SEVENTEEN

"I'm very disappointed in you, Terri," Andy said softly.

The meeting was over. As he'd earlier proposed, Andy'd walked Terri back to her apartment. But it hadn't felt like a casual stroll between friends. It had felt like a jailer escorting a prisoner back to her cell.

Terri stopped herself before she could twist her hands in her lap. She didn't want Andy to know how frightened she was. That would give him an advantage, and he already seemed to be holding all the cards. All the way home from the meeting, he'd given her the cold, silent treatment. As if Doyle's sudden appearance at the meeting had been Terri's fault. Nothing she'd been able to say to the contrary had done any good.

"I don't know why you should be," she answered now. On impulse she decided to stand up. Remaining seated while Andy was standing was making her nervous, not to mention making the wrong impression. It meant he could loom over her, treat her like a child. It wasn't a position she liked. She'd had more than enough of it at home.

"I didn't do anything wrong," she protested, wincing inwardly as she heard how childish it sounded.

Andy folded his arms across his chest. "So you keep saying," he commented. "But I still don't understand how your new friend Doyle"—Andy's tone made the description a sneer, as if the relationship between Terri and Doyle were dirty, somehow—"knew how to find you tonight. Are you quite sure you didn't tell him?"

"I already told you, no," Terri said, her voice rising in spite of her efforts to keep it even and calm. "Of course not. I just met him yesterday, Andy. One of his co-workers lives next door. We all went for a drink and then Doyle asked me out. He wanted to get together again tonight, and I told him I couldn't. I had an important meeting that I couldn't get out of."

"Interesting choice of words," Andy observed. "Didn't you want to come to the meeting, Terri? Aren't you happy with your new life? Your beautiful apartment? Your address book is full of names. You want to go out with a friend? All you have to do is pick up the phone and call one. You don't have to waste your time on a loser like Doyle. But you did. I can't help but wonder why."

Without warning, Terri shivered. Andy's voice was quiet, but she could hear the menace running through it. It was a tone of voice she'd heard him use only once before, with Joy Clement. She moved to the window, putting a little more distance between them.

"I don't understand why you're so angry with me," she said. "I haven't done anything wrong. I came to the meeting. I passed on the Mark."

"That's right, you did," Andy said. "Do you remember the number on the back of the Mark?"

I remember everything about it, Terri thought.

"Three," she whispered, her throat suddenly thick.

"What?" Andy asked. "I didn't quite hear you."

"Three," Terri said.

"And how many days since you passed it on?"

"Two."

"So," Andy said, a cheerful note in his voice. "A little elementary school math tells us that there's still one day to go. Twenty-four hours before your lovely new life is paid for. A lot can happen in a day, Terri. A thing it would be in your best interest to keep in mind."

Terri felt her earlier shiver turn into an uncontrollable tremor, deep within her gut. Andy began to stroll around her apartment, like a real estate agent showing it off.

"Until your new life is truly paid for, all this"—he waved his hand—"can be taken away. *At any time*. If you betray us—if you even mention our name, I'll find out about it. You and anyone you tell will die.

"There's no turning back once you become an Illuminati, Terri. You're in it for life. How long that life lasts is up to you. But you can trust me on one thing. The time of Feutoch is approaching. Very soon now, it will arrive. When it does, I really think you'll want to be one of us."

He's crazy, Terri thought. Aloud she said, "Who's Feutoch?"

Andy's eyes began to glow with a strange fervor. "Feutoch is the one we serve. The one to whom the lives are given. The one who gives us everything we want. Feutoch is the one who makes all things possible. His coming is going to change the world."

Slowly, like a cat stalking its prey, Andy moved across the room to stand in front of her. Every cell in Terri's body screamed at her to move, to get out of range. Only the fact that she knew it would be useless kept her rooted in place. That and the fact that there wasn't any place for her to go.

Andy reached out to capture her chin and hold it still.

"Do you like fire, little Terri Miller?" he asked.

"What?" Terri gasped. She winced as Andy's grip became brutal.

"I said, do you like fire?"

"Yes," Terri answered, her voice no more than a thread of sound.

"Good, that's very good, Terri," Andy said. "Because the time of Feutoch is the time of fire. The world as you know it will come to an end. Only true followers of Feutoch will be spared. All others will perish in the flames. Do you understand?"

Terri opened her mouth to speak, but no sound came out. The only thing she truly understood was that Andy meant every word he said.

Andy's fingers flexed. Sharp pain shot along Terri's jaw. "I didn't quite hear you. I'm afraid you'll have to speak up."

"Yes!" Terri cried. "Yes, I understand. Yes, *yes!*"

"That's better," Andy said. He released her chin and stepped back. Terri locked her knees to keep herself from crumpling to the floor. *Later,* she thought. *You can fall apart later. Don't do it while he's here. Don't give him the satisfaction.*

Andy strolled to the door, put his hand on the knob. At the last second he turned back.

"I wouldn't go to bed too early tonight, if I were you. You might want to stay up and watch the late show. I have it on good authority there's going to be a special broadcast. Right around midnight. If you turn the TV on, you might see someone you know."

He turned the knob, pulled the door open. "Nice chatting with you," Andy said. "I'll see you around. Assuming you're a good girl and do what you've been told."

He stepped into the hall and pulled the door closed behind him with a *click.*

As if the sound released the hidden mechanism that had been holding her up, Terri's knees quivered, then gave way. She sat down, hard, on the floor.

There's no way out, she thought. She'd as good as dug her own grave. There was no one she could turn to for help. If she did, she'd condemn them both. She might not have believed or even understood most of what Andy had said. But she'd believed and understood that much.

Seated on the floor of her beautiful new apartment, the trappings of her dream life all around her, Terri Miller began to laugh.

How in the world could she have been so stupid? she wondered. How could she have believed that things could change? She had a prettier cage now, one she liked much better, but it didn't alter one central truth: She was alone, just the way she'd always been.

"I think I must be hearing things," Doyle said. "Why don't you take me through that again?"

The team was back at Angel Investigations, down in Angel's private quarters. Angel was still unsteady on his feet. Doyle's mood could best be described as foul. A thing which was probably to be expected, under the circumstances. Cordelia had gotten him an ice pack, which he was alternately applying to his left eye and split lip.

"I already told you," Angel said. He wasn't exactly in a sunny mood himself.

To say the evening's activities hadn't gone well was the understatement of a week that had started out bad. They'd been so close. They'd known where the cult was meeting. But with Doyle unconscious and Angel all but out of commission, they hadn't been able to follow up. Instead, they'd been forced to come back to the office to regroup. A thing that wasn't going over very well with anyone.

Doyle removed the ice pack from in front of his mouth. "Tell me again. This time maybe you can include the part about *why* you did it. As in, because you didn't trust me."

"I do trust you," Angel said.

Doyle snorted. "You've got a pretty funny way of showing it. Unless, of course, you do that-thing-you-don't-want-to-talk-about to everyone you trust."

"*Followed you.* I followed you, okay?" Angel said. "It was stupid. I shouldn't have done it. I apologize. I didn't do it because I didn't trust you. I did it because I thought two pairs of eyes might be better than one."

"Too bad neither of you guys saw anything," Cordelia commented from where she sat in between them. A human buffer zone.

Doyle put the ice pack back on his lip. "For your information, I did see something," he announced in a slightly muffled voice. "I got a good luck at the guy Terri was meeting. Real Mr. L.A. type. Said his name was Andy."

"Was this before, during, or after he stuck his fist in your eye?" Cordelia asked.

"Before and during," Doyle replied. "I'm a little hazy about after. That guy's got some anger issues that need to be addressed, you ask me."

"You're sure he wasn't just a jealous boyfriend we didn't know about?" Cordelia pressed.

"Not likely," Angel suddenly spoke up. "My up-close-and-personal was with a representative from our old pals Wolfram and Hart. Add that to Doyle's reception . . ."

"And it sounds like we got a little too close for comfort," Cordelia finished for him.

"Right," Angel said. "Unfortunately, it still doesn't help us much. Aside from Doyle's ability to ID this guy Andy, should he ever run into him again, which doesn't seem likely, we don't know anything we didn't know before."

Except for the fact that Wolfram and Hart wanted him out of the picture in a great big way, a thing he'd decided not to reveal to the others. There was nothing Doyle or Cordelia could do about the fact that he'd been marked. As far as Angel was concerned, that meant they didn't need to know about it.

The three sat silently on the couch for a moment, each lost in his own thoughts.

"How'd he know where to find you?" Doyle finally asked. "The guy from Wolfram and Hart."

"I guess he must have been in on the following act, too," Angel said, after considering the question for a moment. "He can't have known I'd be there ahead of time. *I* didn't even know I'd be there ahead of time."

"Angel, man, show a little mercy. You're making my head hurt worse than it already does."

"Okay, look," Cordelia said, pushing herself to her feet. "We've got to come up with some sort of new plan of action. Time's running out. We can't afford to just sit around nursing our wounds."

"Easy for you to say," Doyle remarked. "You're the only one who hasn't got some."

Cordelia climbed across the coffee table when neither Doyle nor Angel showed much inclination to get out of the way.

"Let's just take stock, okay?" she inquired. "They beat Doyle up," she recapped quickly. "They hit Angel with a tranquilizer dart. These could be good signs. Maybe they're afraid of us."

"Well, it's pretty clear they didn't want us going to the meeting," said Doyle.

"Right, okay, the meeting," Cordelia said.

"What about the meeting? Now we know there was one. That just confirms that Terri's involved with the cult."

"We knew that already, Cordelia," Angel spoke up.

"Well," Cordelia said, her tone exasperated. "Now we really, really know it. We've got to get her to talk. It's our only option. And don't tell me we already knew that, too. Help me out here, guys. I'm trying to get a little positive momentum going."

"We could try surveillance," Doyle suggested. "Never let her out of our sight."

"I don't think so," Angel said. "Remember how well we did the last time."

"I think Doyle should go and talk to her," Cordelia announced. "How do we know that she's all right? Maybe this Andy got rough with her, too. And even if he didn't, Doyle looking the way he does ought to really give us an edge. I'd feel terrible if somebody I knew looked like that."

Doyle took the ice pack down from his face to glare at her. "Somebody you know *does* look like 'that,' Cord."

"And if that doesn't work, I can try," Cordelia said, completely ignoring the sarcasm in Doyle's tone. "In case she's decided you're sneaky, underhanded, and not to be trusted because you followed her, I can provide a sympathetic female-variety shoulder to cry on."

"Actually, it's not a bad plan," Angel commented. He just wished it wasn't their only one. He took his legs off the coffee table, got to his feet. The floor stayed still beneath them. *Good sign.*

"I say we roll with it tonight," Angel went on. "If she's scared, it might be a good time to put the pressure on."

"I don't like it," Doyle said.

"That's because you're emotionally involved."

"I said I thought she was nice," Doyle said, sitting bolt upright. "That doesn't mean I'm emotionally involved. Besides, what the hell would you know about it?"

"Stop it! Just stop it!" Cordelia yelled. "It doesn't matter what you think," she said, jabbing a finger in Angel's direction. "And it doesn't matter if you don't like it," she told Doyle. "What matters is that we work together. If we don't, we might as well just give up and start gathering firewood for Feutoch's big bonfire.

"Personally, I'd rather not do that. One near-end-of-the-world experience was enough for me. But then, I'm not a big macho type like you guys are." She broke off, breathing hard.

"All right," Doyle said. "I'll talk to her tonight."

Angel fished his keys out of his pocket. "I'll drive."

CHAPTER EIGHTEEN

"Terri, are you there? Open up. It's Doyle."

For a moment he was sure she wouldn't answer. Then, "Go away," Terri's voice sounded through the door.

"I can't do that," Doyle said. "You've got to let me in. We've got to talk."

"There's nothing to talk about," Terri's voice sounded again. "Go away, Doyle. I don't want to see you anymore."

They got to her, Doyle thought. He felt something hot and ugly twist deep in his gut. *Bastards. Filthy, rotten fire-demon-loving bastards.* It was bad enough they'd messed with her mind. But if they'd put their hands on her . . .

"I can't do that," he said through the door. "Not until I've seen you. You've got to let me in, Terri. I'm not going anywhere until I know that you're all right."

There was another moment of silence. Then, to his relief, Doyle heard the deadbolt snick back. Terri opened the door. Not wide enough to let him in, just wide enough for her to look out.

"You can see I'm fine," she said. "Now go aw—" As she got a good look at his face, her eyes widened. "Oh, God, they hurt you, Doyle."

She stepped back, involuntarily or on purpose, Doyle couldn't tell. But he was perfectly willing to take advantage of the gesture. He stepped into the apartment and closed the door behind him. He took Terri by the arm, led her back into the living room. She was shaking so badly she could hardly walk. She collapsed onto the couch, doubled over, her face in her hands.

"I'm sorry," she whispered. "I'm so sorry. I didn't know."

Doyle knelt down in front of her. "Don't worry about me," he said. "Believe it or not, I've looked a lot worse. Look at me, Terri. Let me see he didn't touch you." Terri lifted her head. Her face was pale and strained but mostly unmarked. A series of small oval bruises marred one cheek.

Fingerprints, Doyle thought. Too bad he couldn't use them to find out who this Andy really was. He brushed a gentle finger over the bruises. Terri flushed and turned her face aside.

"He didn't hurt you anywhere else, did he?"

Doyle asked. Some guys were smart that way. A sick kind of smart. They only hit women where it didn't show.

"No," Terri managed. "No, he didn't. I'm fine." She pressed her hands to her mouth when she realized what she'd just admitted. "Andy—you're saying Andy did this to you?"

"Who else?" said Doyle.

He rose from his crouch and sat beside Terri.

"But why?" Terri asked. "I don't understand. Why?"

Doyle took one of her hands in his. And took a leap straight out into space. "It's all right, Terri. You don't have to pretend. I know."

Terri's eyes were huge and frightened. "I . . . I don't know what you mean."

"I know about them. About the cult. The Illuminati."

With a sharp cry, Terri yanked her hand away and sprang from the couch. "You can't," she said. "You can't know. I can't talk about them. They said they'd kill me, don't you understand? And they'd kill anyone I—" Horrified, she broke off, breathing hard. "Oh, God," she choked out. "Oh, God, we're both going to die."

Doyle stood up and took her by the shoulders. "Listen to me, Terri," he said. "We are *not* going to die. But only if you help me. You have to tell me what you know."

"I don't know anything," Terri protested wildly.

She shrugged her shoulders, as if trying to throw off his grip. Doyle held on.

"You have to know something," he said. "Or Andy wouldn't have threatened you. Think, Terri. How did you find out about the Illuminati?"

"It was Andy," Terri said. "He found me—that night—in the grocery store parking lot. I was unhappy, so unhappy, and he said that he could make things better. He had a way to make my dreams come true."

"By joining the Illuminati."

Terri nodded. "He said he'd take me to a meeting. We went the very next night."

"He's the leader, isn't he?" Doyle asked.

Again Terri nodded. "I think so. He runs the meetings."

"Where was the first one?" Doyle asked. "The same place as tonight?"

This time Terri shook her head. "It was in some fancy hotel by the ocean. Andy said . . ." She took a shaky breath. "He said they never meet in the same place twice."

Doyle swore.

"Where's the next one?"

Terri's chin wobbled. "I don't know. He said they'd be in touch. He said—" Tears began to slip silently down her pale cheeks. "Please, Doyle, you have to go. I'm not supposed to talk to anyone about any of this. He said they'd *know*."

Doyle guided her back over to the couch,

eased her down. He took a quick turn around the room, his mind working in double time. She'd told him everything she knew, he thought. And it wasn't much. Not nearly enough.

"I want you to come with me," he said. "I can keep you safe."

Once again, Terri bolted from the couch. "No, no! If I leave, they'll know for sure that I've betrayed them. They'll find a way to mark me. I know it."

"They can't mark you if they can't get to you," Doyle said, striving to keep his tone calm. "Terri, you've got to trust me. The only way we can stop them is if all of us who want to work together."

Terri's expression turned bewildered. "What do you mean, all of us who want to stop them? I never said I wanted to do that. I just want to be safe, that's all."

"For crying out loud!" Doyle exploded. "Can't you think about someone other than yourself for one minute? There's more at stake here than just you. The end of the world is coming."

Terri's face went white to the lips. The harsh sound of her breathing was loud in the room. "I don't know what you're talking about."

I've made a mess of this, Doyle thought. "It's why they mark people," he said quietly. "Why the victims all die by fire. They're trying to bring about the end of the world. You've got to help me stop them."

"I don't believe you!" Terri shouted. "I don't know how to stop it. You're no better than they are. Trying to scare me so I'll do what you want." Her movements jerky, Terri dashed toward the door. "I want you to go. You have to go!"

"I can't just leave you unprotected."

Terri put her hand on the doorknob. Her fingers were so slick with nervous sweat they slipped right off. She tried again, gripping it with a conscious effort so hard, the knuckles of her hand turned white.

"You're the one putting me in danger," she said. "I want you to go now, Doyle."

"Come with me," Doyle urged again. "I'll protect you."

"You can't," Terri answered, her tone wooden. She opened the door. Her face set and determined, she looked at Doyle. "Don't come back," she said.

Doyle hesitated a moment, then walked past her into the hall. "You're making a mistake," he said, his voice gentle.

To his surprise, Terri gave a laugh. It had a bitter, hollow sound.

"You know something?" she asked. "That's what people have been telling me my whole life. Looks like joining the Illuminati didn't change anything after all."

She slammed the door closed. Doyle stood in the hall until he heard the deadbolt shoot home.

He'd only taken about two steps before the door to Cordelia's apartment opened.

"Well?" she whispered. "How did it go?"

Doyle covered the rest of the distance before he spoke. "Let me put it this way," he said. "Not well."

Cordelia made a face. "Uh-oh. Want me to go over, see if I can smooth the waters?"

Doyle shook his head. "We push her anymore tonight, she'll fall apart or run. I think we should leave her alone for now. But I'd appreciate it if you'd go over first thing in the morning."

"Will do," Cordelia said. "You're really worried about her, aren't you?"

"She's scared to death, Cordelia. I recognize the signs."

"That makes two of us."

"You wanna stay here tonight?" Cordelia asked. "I can make up the couch."

"No, but thanks," Doyle said. "I need to get out. Get some air. I'll touch base in the morning, all right?"

Doyle left the building, walking quickly. What he needed was a drink, he thought. Something strong and dark and potent. If he was lucky, very lucky, maybe he'd be able to wash the taste of failure from his mouth.

She'd done the wrong thing, Terri thought. Gotten it backward, just like her mother always claimed she did. She'd protected Andy, who wanted to hurt her. Rejected Doyle, who'd wanted to help. He'd claimed that he would keep her safe. She'd known he wanted to. She wondered if he really could.

He'd known about the end of the world.

Clapping a hand across her mouth to keep from crying out, Terri staggered back into the living room. Collapsed on the couch. How had Doyle known? About her involvement with the cult. About the end of the world. All of a sudden, everything about him seemed suspicious. His sudden appearance and interest in her. No guy had ever wanted to take her out before. She'd put Doyle's interest down to her new life. But what if he was someone the Illuminati had sent to spy on her?

She pulled her knees up onto the couch and wrapped her arms around them. Drawing her body into a hard, tight knot of misery. Pressing her back against the cushions of the couch like a prisoner against a wall.

It's what I am, she thought. *What I made myself.*

Her dream of a new life had become a nightmare she had no hope of waking up from.

Abruptly Terri snapped to full attention as an image appeared on the TV screen. She'd turned it on after Andy's departure but kept the volume off. She hadn't wanted to do even that much, but he'd told her to watch, and she'd been afraid to disobey his instructions. Fingers numb, Terri fumbled on the coffee table for the remote control, turned up the volume.

"As frustrated police investigators continue to struggle to identify *him*," the sober-faced television reporter's voice suddenly filled Terri's apartment, "it appears the Krispy Kritter Killer has struck once more. This time his victim is one most of us can easily identify: daytime television star Joy Clement.

"Apparently alone when she was killed in the Beverly Hills mansion she'd only recently purchased, Ms. Clement's death brings the total number of deaths attributed to the Krispy Kritter to seventeen. As the death count rises, angry, frightened citizens' groups are putting pressure on city hall. Their message: Do whatever it takes to end the fiery reign of terror. Police Chief—"

Terri punched the mute button, and the television set fell silent. But she continued to stare at the images flickering on the screen. They were all of Joy Clement. Early pictures of her as a struggling young summer-stock actress gradually gave way to more recent ones. Finally there was a shot of her at the banquet where she'd won her recent award.

The expression on Joy's face as she made her acceptance speech made Terri's eyes hurt. Her smile was so dazzling it was like looking into the sun. How long after that moment had Joy developed her first doubts? Terri wondered. How long before she'd realized she'd flown as high as she could go, and the only thing left was to come back down?

Without warning, Terri felt her skin go clammy with horror. Joy Clement had known she was going to die. She herself had heard Joy tell Andy she could no longer pay the price the Illuminati required. She'd all but begged him to put her out of her misery. Obviously, he'd been more than happy to comply.

With a shock Terri realized that she was weeping, silently. Joy had tried to warn others, while Terri was nothing but a coward. She'd had a chance, and she'd thrown it all away. She hadn't trusted Doyle. Instead, she'd sent him away. As he'd claimed, she'd thought only of herself.

It wasn't going to matter. Not for very much longer. She knew that now. That was the message Andy had wanted to give her. The reason he'd wanted her to turn on the television.

Like Joy Clement, she was going to die.

CHAPTER NINETEEN

Septimus was feeling strange. Calm and desperate, all at the same time. He knew he wanted to find Terri. But there were moments when he couldn't remember why. The last few days had begun to run together. The images distorting, bleeding into one another like sidewalk chalk pictures disintegrating in a sudden rainstorm.

The only good things were that he was back in a neighborhood he recognized. Back to where he'd started. That and the five-dollar bill he'd found. He'd seen the guy who'd dropped it. But when Septimus had called out, determined to return it to him, determined not to take anything else that didn't rightfully belong to him, the guy had freaked and run away.

Only then did Septimus begin to feel right. He'd done the right thing, giving the envelope back. He'd tried to give the guy back his five spot.

But he'd been turned down. Rewarded for his willingness to make a sacrifice. It was the next sign, he thought. He was going to find Terri. It was just a matter of time.

He stood on the sidewalk, considering what to do next. Food, he thought. Not from some restaurant. Five dollars barely bought you coffee and a muffin in L.A. Besides, going to a restaurant wouldn't help him find Terri. But he knew something that might.

Stuffing the bill into the same pocket in which he'd earlier carried the precious envelope, Septimus set off toward the grocery store where Terri liked to shop. It was night, the time she liked to go. If his luck had truly changed, that's where he would find her.

"Slow down, Andy. We need to talk."

At the sound of the voice behind him, Andy started, then swung around. Dammit! He was getting jumpy. And even worse, he'd shown it. He could tell himself it was because it was late and he was tired. But even he wouldn't believe it, not entirely. He'd made a mistake about Terri Miller. A big one. He couldn't quite shake the feeling that it was going to cost him.

He narrowed his eyes, taking in the guy whose voice had stopped him as he'd walked down the sidewalk on the way to his apartment. He knew him, Andy realized. He was a new member of the

Illuminati, part of the same meeting that had recruited Terri Miller. One of the few new members Andy hadn't vetted first.

"I know you," he said. "Your name is—"

The other guy's lips quirked upward in a smile. "I believe the name I gave was John. John Smith."

It was time to reassert his authority, Andy thought. Reassert control. "You were supposed to be at a meeting tonight, *John*," he said. "There are rules, you know. If you want to stay alive, you'll play by them."

To Andy's astonishment, John Smith threw back his head and laughed.

"Save it," he said. "Not that I don't appreciate the show. I was doing something much more important tonight than testifying about the Illuminati."

"Such as?"

"Let's just say I was doing a little troubleshooting," John Smith answered. "After all, the fact that I didn't attend your little meeting doesn't mean our interests aren't the same."

"And those interests are?"

John Smith smiled. The sight reminded Andy of a predator after a satisfying snack. A really warm-blooded one that had bled a lot.

"Making sure Feutoch gets what he wants. I hate to tell you this, Andy, but you've got a big problem on your hands. Fortunately, I think I can help you solve it."

Andy felt his instincts go on red alert. What was going on here? Had he flushed out the Summoner?

Cult rank-and-file members weren't given full info on the fire demon. They were told only the basics of how the cult functioned. The benefits they would receive when they joined. But John Smith knew about Feutoch. How had he come by his information? Andy wondered.

"I don't know what you're talking about," Andy said. "I don't have a problem."

John Smith flicked an imaginary piece of lint from the arm of his suit coat. "Have it your way," he said. "You don't want to talk, you might want to listen. Knowledge is power, after all."

Andy was silent.

John Smith gave a tight smile. "Some of the news is good," he went on. "We're closer than you think, you know. To the change. The great conflagration of Feutoch. By my calculations, he could reach his count as soon as tomorrow night, assuming there are no unforeseen complications, of course."

Andy's heart began to pound in hard, swift strokes. "How do you know that?"

Smith shrugged. "Let's just say I have my sources. You have to be careful about taking people at face value, Andy. That could have unfortunate consequences."

Abruptly Andy felt his temper snap. He took two quick steps forward, his hand snaking out to wrap around John Smith's tie as he yanked him to his toes.

"Keep on threatening me," he said, his voice low and feral, "and you'll be feeling some unexpected consequences of your own."

John's expression never faltered, even as his face turned an unnatural red. "Let's talk about Terri Miller first."

"What about her?" Andy growled.

John rolled his eyes down toward Andy's clenched fist. As abruptly as he'd struck, Andy released him. John faltered back a step. He took a moment to straighten his tie before he replied.

"Terri Miller has a friend."

"Doyle," Andy said. "I know. I've met him. After the reception he got, I don't think he'll be a problem."

"I suggest you think again. He left Terri's apartment a little after eleven. Correct me if I'm wrong, but I believe that would be *after* you were there."

Andy felt a spurt of adrenaline shoot straight down his spine. "Terri Miller isn't going to say jack," he said roughly. "She's going to do exactly what I tell her. She knows she'll be dead if she doesn't."

"I certainly hope so. The trouble is, Doyle's not a lone agent. He has help that could seriously jeopardize our plans. I've taken steps to neutralize that threat. You should do the same with the one Terri Miller poses. Leaving her on her own isn't smart."

Andy clenched his teeth. "I'll take care of it," he promised.

"Glad to hear it," Smith said. "I hear she has an interesting habit. When she gets upset, she goes grocery shopping."

"I said I'd take care of it," Andy snapped.

John Smith smiled. "In that case, Andy, let me just say I'll look forward to seeing you in hell."

Terri wasn't sure just when she decided to go to the grocery store. All she'd known was that she couldn't stay in the apartment one moment longer. It wasn't until she was actually pulling into the parking lot that she realized what she'd done: returned to the thing she'd tried to leave behind. How much more pathetic could she get? she wondered.

She switched the engine off and sat for a moment. Would it still work? The bright calmness of walking up and down the aisles. If she went inside, would she be able to forget all the things she'd done, even if only for a few moments?

It wasn't until she was almost to the front entrance that she realized she'd sought her own version of sanctuary too late.

Andy was waiting for her, right outside the doors.

*   *   *

Terri was in some kind of trouble. Septimus was sure of it. It was all falling into place now. All the things that he had been through. All the signs. There was a reason he hadn't been able to find her before. She hadn't needed him enough. But she needed him now.

He'd been so excited when he'd seen her walking toward the store. At last, all his hardships were going to pay off. Nobody had noticed him, standing by the big ice freezers just inside the front door. When she came in, Terri was going to walk right by him. She would recognize him. She would smile.

"Hello, Septimus," she'd say. "I'm so glad to see you."

She never even made it in the door.

The guy outside, he wouldn't let her in. Terri was afraid of him. Septimus could tell. Her face had a funny pinched expression, one he'd never seen before.

She's frightened, he thought. As he watched, Terri's footsteps faltered and came to a halt. The guy moved toward her and took her arm. Septimus could see his lips moving rapidly, but he couldn't hear what he was saying. Not from inside the store.

Without warning, Terri tried to pull back, and the guy gave her arm a quick brutal jerk. Septimus saw Terri cry out. In the next moment the guy was hurrying her away, holding her arm at a funny angle. The same way Septimus's father had when Septimus was a child and his dad had made him go somewhere he didn't want to. He could still remember how that had felt.

He's hurting her, he thought.

He hurried from the store. He expected the guy to get into a car, but he didn't. Instead, walking quickly, he began to hustle Terri down the sidewalk.

It's all right, Terri, Septimus thought. *I'll stay with you. I won't let you be alone.* That's what had always happened when his dad had pulled his arm like that. Septimus had ended up in the dark. Alone.

But that wasn't going to happen to Terri. Not if Septimus could help it. Pulling his coat more tightly around him, he began to follow. Began to walk once more.

"How'd it go?" Angel asked.

He and Doyle were in Angel's office, the same room where the team had originally met with Deirdre Arensen. The overhead light was on, the blinds drawn to keep out the morning sunshine.

"Not very well," Doyle said. He scrubbed a hand across his face, then winced. The hits he'd taken the night before were still painful. He hadn't slept well.

"I don't think he roughed her up, but Andy

definitely messed with her head. Terri Miller was scared to death last night. Kept going on about how talking to me would put me in danger. I tried to get her to come here, come with me, but she wouldn't go for it. Finally she got so freaked that I did what she asked."

"Which was?"

"Exit stage right." Doyle made a frustrated sound. "Cordy's checking on her now. You know—in the light of day?"

"Not lately," Angel said. There was an awkward moment of silence. "Doyle—"

"Forget about it," Doyle swiftly interrupted. He'd had most of the night to reflect on Angel's actions of the day before and what he had to figure were their true causes. "This Feutoch thing has us all on edge. You were only trying to do what was right."

"Too bad it turned out to be so pathetic."

Without warning, Doyle gave a wolfish grin. "Oh, I don't know. I've always been a fan of the Keystone Cops, myself."

"More like the Three Stooges," Angel said. "It was a good idea, though."

"What?"

"Trying to get Terri Miller to come here. That might have turned the tables. Made them come to us, for a change."

"Maybe Cordelia will come through."

"Maybe," Angel said.

Abruptly Angel smacked his open palm against the wall hard enough to make it shake. "Dammit!" he yelled. "We're practically at ground zero, and all we have are the same loose ends we've had all along. If we can't weave them into something coherent before midnight tonight, Deirdre Arensen is going to wake up dead."

Angel reached for the phone.

"What are you doing?"

"Calling Deirdre. Getting her down here," Angel replied. "I want sort of a final planning session before tonight. Maybe I can finally convince her to give up that damned Mark of Feutoch." Having another couldn't hurt him, since he'd already been marked. But convincing Deirdre to give up hers could still save her life.

"Good luck," said Doyle.

Angel pulled Deirdre's business card out of his shirt pocket and dialed the phone. He put his hand over the receiver to speak to Doyle.

"She's not there," he said. He removed his hand. "Deirdre, this is Angel," he said as the answering machine completed its recorded message. "I think we should meet. Call me when you get in." He hurled the phone back into its cradle. "Things continue to go our way," he remarked.

Whatever Doyle might have replied was interrupted by the sound of footsteps, hurrying down the hall. A moment later, Cordelia burst in. One look at her face informed Doyle and Angel that something was very definitely wrong.

"It's Terri, isn't it?" Doyle asked. "What is it? Is she hurt?"

"I don't know," Cordelia said. "She's gone."

CHAPTER TWENTY

"Gone? What do you mean she's gone?" Stunned, Doyle sank down till his butt rested on the edge of Cordelia's desk.

"I mean she's gone," Cordelia repeated. "What part of that can you possibly fail to understand?"

"What happened, Cord?" Angel broke in.

"I went over, first thing this morning. Terri didn't answer the door. I went to the super. Said I was worried that Terri wasn't answering because we'd planned to ride to work together. He didn't want to let me in, but I convinced him eventually."

"And?" Doyle prompted.

"And she was *gone*. But it was weird. All the lights in the living room were on. So was the TV, but the sound was off. Her bed hadn't been slept in. It's like she just stepped out."

"Or was taken out," Angel countered. "Did you check the parking garage?"

Cordelia nodded. "Her car wasn't in her spot."

"So it's possible she took off on her own."

"Possible, but doubtful," Cordelia said. "When the super wasn't looking, I did some snooping around. The bedroom is still full of her clothes. She had nice things, Angel. Not designer, but good quality. Expensive. No girl in her right mind is going to take off and leave a closet full of silk behind."

"Andy got to her," Doyle said. "He was afraid she'd talk, so he took her out of the picture. It's the only thing that adds up."

Angel nodded, his expression grim. "I'm afraid you're right. Though I think we can assume she's safe for the time being. He wouldn't want to hurt her right away."

All three members of Angel Investigations fell silent, as they all mentally contemplated the thing no one was willing to say. The reason Terri Miller was still safe was that there was only one way her death would benefit the cult. If she became a victim of Feutoch.

"Well," Doyle said at last. "At least we're still on the same time frame."

Cordelia jumped as the phone on her desk shrilled. She walked to it, picked it up. "Angel Investigations. We help the helpless. How can we—what? Yes, yes, he's here. Hold on." She turned to face Doyle and Angel. "It's Deirdre Arensen," she mouthed.

"Deirdre, where are you?" Angel asked as Cordelia handed him the phone. "I left a message at your place."

"I'm on my way to your office," Deirdre's voice said. She sounded energized. Excited. "Angel, I think I've got something. Ellen Bradshaw came through from beyond the grave."

"How?" Angel asked.

"She sent me a photograph of the cult leader. I don't know why it took so long to arrive. I know who it is, Angel. I recognize him. I'll explain when I get there. But we can do it now. We can stop them."

Five minutes later Deirdre tossed a battered manila envelope onto the table with a soft slap.

"That was in my P.O. box when I checked it first thing this morning. It was sent to me by Ellen Bradshaw. It's postmarked the day after her death."

"The mailbox," Angel said. "Ellen Bradshaw died right by a mailbox.

"Apparently, not a coincidence." Deirdre nodded. She took the photo from the envelope and placed it faceup on the table. "That's him," she said. "That's the cult leader."

"Damn," Angel said quietly.

"I thought you'd think so."

Angel's eyes shot to Doyle's. "Is this him?" he asked. "Is this the one who rearranged your face?"

Doyle leaned over. "That's Andy," he said. He looked from Angel to Deirdre, his expression puzzled. "How come you guys are acting like you know him?"

"Because we do," Deirdre said. "That's Jackson Tucker, the detective in charge of the Krispy Kritter investigation."

"Oh, shit," Doyle said.

"There's more," Deirdre went on, her eyes on Angel. "Something I haven't told you. Kate wanted me to. I guess she was right. I'd just like to say in advance that I'm sorry."

"What is it?" Angel asked.

"When I got home from your office, that first day, Tucker was waiting for me. He said the interview with Ellen Bradshaw's parents had made him reconsider my story. Ellen's mother had hinted her daughter might be involved in a cult."

"So all of a sudden Tucker wanted to pick your brain."

Deirdre nodded. "He was very persuasive," she said. "And I—I fell for it. I let him see some of my father's files."

"Did you tell him that you'd come to me?"

"No. And I didn't tell him I'd been marked."

There was a beat of silence. "I told you," Deirdre said, her voice defensive. "I told you up front that I would do whatever it took to find those responsible for what happened to my father. I couldn't send Tucker away. Not if I thought he could help."

"Looks like you helped him, instead."

Deirdre flushed. "Look, I said that I was sorry. I'm going to hate it when Kate finds out about this. She always claimed I was too personally involved."

Deirdre looked at the three sober faces surrounding her, in turn. "So, what do we do now?"

"Thanks for the coffee, Dad," Kate said. "I'd better get back. You should see the mountain of paperwork on my desk."

It wasn't often her father, a retired cop and the reason Kate had wanted to join the force in the first place, showed up at his old stomping grounds. According to him, there was nothing worse than a retired cop who couldn't stay retired. Kate figured he'd shown up today as a show of support. Things had been tough enough before, but Joy Clement's death had made things a whole lot worse.

It was a cop credo that every murder victim, every victim for that matter, deserved the same thing: justice. It was also a fact of life that the population at large, to say nothing of the media, reacted more strongly when bad things happened to famous people.

"So, how's Ol' Hick handling things?" her father asked as they left the coffee shop and walked back toward the office.

Kate shot a puzzled glance in her father's direction. He had to be talking about Tucker, though he'd gotten the nickname wrong. "I didn't know you knew him," she said.

"I don't—not really," her father answered. "Just by reputation. And his captain back East is a pretty good friend."

"How come you called him Old Hick?" Kate asked. "Tucker's not any older than I am. And besides, it's the Hick, not Old Hick."

Her father shook his head. "Don't you young people know anything about history?" he asked. "How do you think he got the nickname in the first place?"

"Because of what he looks like," Kate explained. "You know, sort of reverse psychology."

"Where in hell did you get that idea?" her father asked. "It's because of his name, Katie. Andrew Jackson Tucker."

"So?"

Her father rolled his eyes. "You *have* heard of Andrew Jackson, seventh president of the United States? Old Hickory was a nickname he acquired during the War of 1812. Preston, Detective Tucker's former captain, is a history buff. When he found out what Tucker's full name was, he started calling him Ol' Hick. Guess the name stuck."

"Ever thought about going on *Jeopardy*?" Kate asked. "I swear, Dad, the things you know."

Her father shrugged. "I got a cop's brain for

details, that's all." They reached his car. He took his keys from his pocket and unlocked the driver's door. "Bet he hates it that you guys call him *the* Hick."

"You don't think we're stupid enough to do it to his face, do you?" Kate inquired.

Her father grinned, then sobered. "Catch this guy, Katie," he said.

"I'm sure Tucker's working on it, Dad," Kate answered. "Thanks for stopping by. I'll see you around."

She watched as he got into the car, started it up, drove off. As she made her way back to her desk, Kate found herself wondering what else about Detective Andrew Jackson Tucker she didn't know.

Terri came to in the dark.

Andy'd given her something to make her sleep, so she couldn't run away. But he'd taped her mouth first, she remembered. Then, when she'd been unable to plead with him not to, he'd taped her eyes. She could feel the way the duct tape wound around her head. The way the sticky thickness of it pressed against her closed eyelids.

Where am I? she thought. Something about the way the air around her felt gave Terri the impression of space. Was she in a warehouse? She thought she must be tied to a chair. She couldn't feel her arms or legs, but she was sitting up.

Why had Andy taken her, then left her like this? Had he left her here to starve?

Terri began to struggle against the strips of tape that bound her hands, and succeeded only in sending shooting pains up and down both arms. *Don't panic*, she told herself. Besides, she remembered now. Andy hadn't left her here to starve. The death he'd arranged would be quicker, and much more brutal.

He'd marked her, just as he had Joy Clement. He'd put the Mark in her right shoe.

Doyle, Terri thought. Had Andy gone after him? She had no way of knowing. Just as she had no way of knowing if Doyle himself even knew that she was gone. Would he come back to her apartment? Would he search for her when he discovered she was gone?

She knew it was ridiculous to hope, probably futile to pray. But the truth was, she simply couldn't help herself. *Please*, she thought. *I may deserve it, but don't let me die like this. Let Doyle come for me. Let him be in time.*

Septimus was waiting. Biding his time. He knew Terri was inside the big building somewhere, but he couldn't get in. The man who'd taken her had been too fast for him. He'd closed the door before Septimus could get inside. Septimus was afraid to challenge him directly. The man looked fit and strong.

He had to figure the man was coming back, though. He'd gone to a lot of trouble to bring Terri here. It didn't make sense to Septimus that he would just go off and leave her for too long.

He settled down to wait. He would use the time to marshal his strength. When the guy came back, Septimus intended to be ready for him.

"Okay," Angel said. "Here's how it's going to go. Tucker's not the only one who can run a smokescreen. You"—he pointed at Deirdre—"are going to give him a call. You've just received new information that could lead directly to the cult's downfall."

"Are you out of your mind?" Deirdre said. "You want me to tell him what we know?"

"No," Angel answered, his tone making it quite clear the matter was not open to discussion. "I want you to tell him you know *something*, and to give him the *impression* that you'll tell him what you know. Say he has to see what you've uncovered in person. You can't communicate it over the phone. Then set up a meeting. Make it for late tonight."

"Let me guess. Just before midnight, right?"

"You catch on. When he shows up, we plant the Mark of Feutoch on him."

"How?" Deirdre asked. "You haven't got one."

Do so, Angel thought. Though he kept the information to himself. "I will in a minute," he said aloud. "You're going to give me yours."

"Now, wait just a minute . . ." Deirdre protested.

"No, *you* wait a minute." Three heads swiveled toward the unexpected sound of Cordelia's voice. "You came to Angel because you wanted his help. As far as I can see, all you've done is screw things up. Personally, I'd do what he wants. Otherwise, we'll find a way to handle this on our own. You need us. We don't need you."

"Nice job, Cord," murmured Doyle.

"I—" Deirdre said. "Oh, all right, for crying out loud. You want a ticket to die, that's your business."

She thrust a hand into her purse, pulled the Mark out, and slapped it down onto the tabletop. Without a word Angel picked it up and pocketed it.

"I sure hope this means you've figured out a way to put the fire demon out when he shows."

Angel picked up the receiver and held it out toward Deirdre. "Make the call."

CHAPTER TWENTY-ONE

It's okay. Everything's okay, Tucker told himself. Sure, he had a lot of balls in the air, and he was starting to feel the strain of keeping them up. It would be fatal to drop even one. But now that he was actually on his way to the meeting with Deirdre, he was feeling better. It didn't matter what she knew. Come midnight, there'd be absolutely nothing she could do about it.

He hung a left, silently cruising down the row of warehouses, eyes searching out the one where Deirdre's father, Martin Arensen, had lost his life. It had been an eerie coincidence, Deirdre's demanding a meeting in this place. Did she know about Terri Miller? he wondered. Was this the information she claimed to have? Terri's abduction and the place she was being held?

No, that couldn't be it, he decided. It had to be something more.

"I know," Deirdre had said. "I've found the way to bring the cult down."

A meeting tonight, at a location she specified, just before midnight, was the only way that she would tell him. *Insufferable bitch,* Tucker thought. Well, she would pay. She'd find out soon enough she wasn't so smart. He was going to enjoy watching.

He located the building, pulled around to the back. He was just getting out of the car when he heard a squeal of tires. A moment later Deirdre's car jerked to a stop beside his. She shot from the driver's seat like she'd been fired from a gun.

"Thank God you're here," she said. To his surprise, she clung to his arm. It was the first time he'd ever seen her lose her nerve. He gave in to the impulse to pull her into his arms.

"It's okay. You're safe now. What is it? What's wrong?"

Deirdre's body gave one last tremor, then was still.

"I'm not sure but—I think they may have followed me here," she said. "We should get inside."

"Pretty weird, huh?" Doyle asked from his position in the passenger seat of Angel's car. They were parked some distance away, had been for quite some time. Close enough to keep an eye on the warehouse, not so close to be noticed.

"What do you mean?" Angel asked.

"Deirdre's pickin' this spot for the meeting. You know, where her dad bought it."

"I think it's a thing called closure."

From the backseat Cordelia gave a sniff. "Well, I think it's morbid. Deirdre's going to need some major therapy when all this is over, if you ask me." A beat of silence filled the interior of the convertible. "Assuming that she's still alive, of course."

Angel tensed as a car pulled in behind the warehouse, and a single occupant got out. "Heads up, guys," he advised.

"That's him," Doyle said.

A moment later a second car arrived with a screech of brakes.

"I'll say this much for her," Cordelia said. "She's right on time."

The three watched as Deirdre bolted from the car, all but throwing herself into Tucker's arms.

"Hamming it up a little, wouldn't you say?" murmured Doyle.

"Quiet," Angel said. Silently they watched as Tucker ushered Deirdre through the back door of the warehouse. Angel opened the car door.

"Okay," he said. "Looks like it's showtime. You guys all clear on what to do?"

"Oh, absolutely," said Doyle.

"Actually," Cordelia said. "I'm a little fuzzy on one thing. The whether-or-not-this-is-going-to-work part."

❋   ❋   ❋

Tucker took Deirdre by the arm and pulled her inside the warehouse. "What the hell do you mean, you think you're being followed? You didn't lead anybody here, did you?"

"I don't know," Deirdre said. Tucker swore. "No, no, I don't think so. It was just this feeling. I've had it all day, ever since I called you. I'm probably just being paranoid."

"Let's hope so," Tucker said. He snapped on a flashlight.

"Can't we turn a light on?" Deirdre asked. "I— I don't like the dark."

"I don't have time to pamper you, Deirdre," Tucker said. "Just tell me what I need to know."

"Damn you," Deirdre said fiercely. "I want to see your face. I don't tell you anything in the dark."

Tucker mumbled something beneath his breath. "Suit yourself."

The flashlight moved away. Deirdre heard a loud *click,* like the sound of a circuit-breaker switch. A powerful bank of overhead lights switched on. She lifted a hand to cover her eyes.

"You asshole." She took her hand down from her eyes, faced Tucker as he stood against the wall. "But then, what can I expect from the man who's responsible for condemning at least seventeen innocent people to death?"

Tucker's face blanched, but he held his ground. "What the hell is that supposed to mean?"

"You know what it means . . . *Andy,*" Deirdre

went on. "Remember victim number fourteen? Ellen Bradshaw? I'm afraid you didn't get to her quite fast enough. Ellen sent me a picture before she died. A picture she swore was of the cult leader. You're very photogenic."

"This is pathetic," Tucker said. "You drag me out here in the middle of the night to accuse me? It's obviously an attempt by the cult to discredit me. I'm the one *leading* the investigation. I'm an obvious target."

"It's been convenient for you, hasn't it?" Deirdre asked, completely ignoring his denial. "Nobody ever thought to question the integrity of the dedicated Detective Tucker. You son of a bitch! You killed my father! I'm not going to let you get away with it."

Without warning, Tucker laughed. "I just love it when people say that. Particularly when they're wrong. I *am* going to get away with this. It's all in place. Everything I need is right here in this warehouse."

"What do you mean?"

"Look behind you."

Deirdre turned. In the center of the warehouse was a young woman, bound hand and foot to a chair.

"What have you done?" Deirdre shouted.

"At least we get to go in the front this time," Cordelia whispered as she and Doyle made their way around the side of the warehouse. Each was carrying a bulky satchel.

"I went in the front last time," Doyle replied. "It's overrated, let me tell you."

Together, they rounded the corner of the building. Swiftly Doyle moved to where the metal door that made up most of the front of the warehouse was padlocked. Angel had gotten it right, he thought. The lock was cheap, and small. He knelt in front of it, removing a pair of bolt cutters from the satchel.

"What do we do if somebody comes along and wants to know what we're doing here?" Cordelia asked suddenly.

Doyle gave a grunt as he applied the cutters to the lock. "We're trying to save the world here, Cord. Tell them to back off."

Tucker had moved to the center of the warehouse, beside his prisoner. In a parody of a gesture by a lover, he stroked a hand across her hair. The woman made a choked sound and tried to pull her head away. Tucker pulled her head back toward him with a vicious yank. In the harsh glare of the overhead light, Deirdre could see that the other woman's eyes and mouth were taped shut.

"Let's just call this job security," Tucker said. "Circumstances compel me to relate that Terri Miller here"—he gave her head another jerk—"is one of my very few mistakes. I made an error in judging her character. I thought she was such a desperate little nobody she'd never question all the lovely things being a cult member could give her. Unfortunately, she turned out to have just a little bit more backbone than I expected.

"I couldn't leave her on her own. She could spoil everything I've worked so hard for."

"If she won't, I will," a new voice said.

Deirdre spun toward the sound. "Jeez, Angel. What took you so long?" she said.

Tucker released Terri and began to reach for his shoulder holster.

"He's got a gun!" Deirdre cried.

"He's a cop. Of course he's got a gun."

Tucker freed the gun from the holster.

"Deirdre, get down!" Angel shouted. He launched himself through the air. He heard a bullet whine by his head as he toppled Deirdre, protecting her from the hard concrete of the warehouse floor with his own body as he rolled. He let his momentum carry them both to one side, then scrambled to his feet, pulling Deirdre up behind him.

"I don't know who you are," Tucker said. "But you are definitely going to die."

"I wouldn't be too sure," Angel answered. "I'm harder to kill than I look."

The reply Tucker might have made was interrupted by a strange new sound. It reminded Angel of an animal caught in a trap. Part keen of pain. Part feral growl. Hearing it made the hairs on the back of his neck stand on end. He felt a rush of air go past him as the thing making the sound charged across the warehouse. Tucker fired a second time. The thing staggered back, then kept on going. With a flying tackle, he brought Tucker down.

It's a man, Angel thought. A shambles of a man, dressed in an oversize camouflage overcoat. He was bigger than Tucker, fighting like a madman. But Angel could already tell the way that this would go.

It only took moments for Tucker's combat instincts to kick in. He rammed the butt end of his gun into the guy's shoulder. Howling in agony, the guy in the overcoat loosed his hold. Tucker punched up, catching him right underneath the jaw. His body arced up. The second he was out from underneath, Tucker attacked. Straddling his opponent, pistol-whipping him across the face. The guy in the overcoat got in one more blow, then lay still.

Panting with exertion, Tucker scrambled to his feet, turning back toward Angel and Deirdre.

"Stay behind me," Angel murmured.

Slowly Tucker began to pace across the warehouse toward Angel and Deirdre. He held the gun out in front of him. Angel's whole body itched with the need to attack. *Be patient. Wait for him,* he schooled himself. He had absolutely no intention of continuing to stand here, providing an unmoving target. But if he launched his own attack too soon, he'd leave Deirdre exposed.

Tucker continued his stalk across the warehouse. With his free hand, he gave his jacket a tug, as if to straighten it, offended that the fight had mussed up his clothing. As he did so, something tumbled to the ground. It hit the concrete floor of the warehouse with a metallic *ping*.

Tucker stopped walking abruptly.

The thing rolled in a circle once, twice, then lay still. In the stark light of the warehouse it was impossible to miss what it was: the Mark of Feutoch. Behind him, Angel felt Deirdre Arensen stiffen.

His breath coming fast, Tucker stared down at the Mark. Then he lifted his eyes. For a moment Angel thought the other man was looking at him. Then he realized Tucker's attention was focused behind him, on Deirdre Arensen.

"You did this," Tucker said in a strangled voice. "You marked me. It has to be you. I'm careful. Always so careful. But I let you get close. It was that clinging-violet routine, wasn't it? That was clever, I have to admit. You knew I'd enjoy seeing you helpless."

"I don't know what you're talking about," Deirdre said.

All of a sudden Tucker began to laugh. "My God," he said. "I thought I'd been so smart, but you've done me one better. You're the Summoner, aren't you? That's the only thing that makes sense. The only way you could have the Mark and know what it does. You're not a cult member. If you were, I'd know it. That means you have to be the Summoner."

"You're crazy," Deirdre choked out.

"Oh, I don't think so," Tucker said, his voice turning hard. "I think my version works just fine. You call me up, get me to come down here . . ."

Swiftly Deirdre stepped out from behind Angel, putting some space between them. "That was his idea." She pointed.

Tucker shot Angel a look of sympathy. "Fooled you, too, didn't she?" he asked. "Got you to be her knight in shining armor."

Angel reached into his pocket, held an object out toward Deirdre. "This is the Mark you were so reluctant to part with, the one I insisted you give me earlier today. Where did the one on Tucker come from?"

"For Pete's sake, Angel," Deirdre protested. "You can't believe this guy! He's as good as admitted he's the cult leader. He'll say anything to get himself off the hook."

"Who recruited you, Detective Tucker?" Angel asked suddenly. Beside him, he heard Deirdre suck in a breath.

Tucker gave a nasty smile. "Ask her," he said, jerking his chin in Deirdre's direction. "Though you look like a guy who knows his way around. I'll bet you can figure it out. I was recruited by the only person she could trust enough to help her get the whole ball rolling. Someone who loved her enough to do whatever she wanted.

"Tell me something, Deirdre," Tucker went on, his tone conversational. "Did your father know what would happen after he'd outlived his usefulness? Or did you let him go in blind? But then, he never really did outlive his usefulness, did he? You gained so much from dear old Daddy's death."

"You go to hell!" Deirdre shouted.

"Undoubtedly, I will," Tucker said. "But I'm going to make sure I don't go alone."

With one sudden movement he dived for the Mark. As soon as he saw Tucker move, Angel lunged. Not toward Tucker, but toward Terri Miller. Tucker scooped up the Mark, rose to his feet, and jerked the unprotected Deirdre Arensen into his arms. Deirdre fought like an animal. Kicking. Biting. Clawing. Tucker backhanded her across the face, and she stopped struggling.

"This is going to hurt," Angel said to the young woman. "I'm sorry." Terri let out a scream of pain as he tore the strip of duct tape from her mouth. "Where did he mark you?" Angel rapped out. "Where's the amulet, Terri? Can you tell me?"

"Shoe—right—shoe—" Terri gasped.

Angel yanked the shoe off. The Mark of Feutoch tumbled to the floor.

Without warning, Angel felt the air around him change. Felt the way it thickened, grew still and close and hot. He knew what that meant. There was only one thing it *could* mean.

The hour of the demon had come.

"Now!" Angel shouted.

There was a shrieking grind of metal. Then, slowly, the big metal warehouse door began to travel upward. Feutoch continued to manifest, the very air compressing, folding in upon itself until it took on shape and form. Sparks danced. There was a distinct smell of sulfur. And then, with a surge of heat so strong it had Angel lifting an arm to shield his face, Feutoch materialized in the warehouse.

His fiery body reached halfway to the ceiling. Within it, Angel could see that eerie human outline. The eyes, impossibly pure as crystal in the writhing, twisting tongues of flame.

The warehouse door finished its ascent. Doyle and Cordelia stepped into the warehouse, their satchels in their hands.

There was a pause.

Then Feutoch, the fire demon, spoke. His voice the sound of water being poured upon hot coals. Angel felt the hiss of it reverberate along his spine. He shivered, even though he wasn't cold.

"More than one is marked here," the demon said. "But not all will suit my cause."

"I was hoping you'd feel that way," Angel said. For one moment his gaze met that of Deirdre Arensen. There was blood on her lip from where Tucker had struck her. She stared back at Angel with a tiny furrow between her brows. Angel returned his attention to the fire demon. He could see something flicker in the back of Feutoch's ice-clear eyes. *Curiosity,* he thought.

"You pass among them freely, yet they do not fear you," the demon said. "Do they not know what you are?"

Angel shrugged. "Some do, some don't," he replied.

"Interesting," the demon commented. "But I'm sure you'll understand if I don't chat longer. I come into my own tonight. I've waited a long time. I'd rather not wait any longer."

"Knock yourself out," Angel said.

"Angel, no!" Deirdre shouted.

She made a last, desperate attempt to free herself. Twisting wildly, Deirdre broke Tucker's hold. She hurled herself to one side just as long tongues of flame from Feutoch began to lick toward them. Tucker lunged after Deirdre. Catching her by one leg, he brought them both crashing to the warehouse floor.

"You won't escape, you bitch," he panted. "If I go down, you go with me."

Deirdre lashed out with one foot, catching Tucker full in the face. Still, he did not relinquish his hold. He pinned her legs beneath his body, lying on top of her in some weird parody of a lover's embrace. Deirdre began to laugh, the sound strained and wild.

"He won't hurt me. He needs me. But all of you are expendable. I'll watch you die."

"I wouldn't be too sure of that, if I were you," the demon said. With a burst of heat like a blast furnace, he engulfed them both.

"Ready!" Angel shouted.

"Aim!" called Doyle. He pulled a heavy-duty fire extinguisher from his satchel, lobbed it to Angel. Cordy pulled one from her satchel just as Doyle pulled out one of his own. As if they were one person, the three raised the big, black nozzles of the extinguishers, aiming them straight at Feutoch.

"Fire!" Angel yelled. White clouds belched forth from the mouths of the fire extinguishers. As they hit his fiery body, Feutoch sent up an unearthly howl. Tongues of flame shot straight up toward the roof. Thick clouds of acrid smoke filled the warehouse.

"Keep going!" Angel shouted.

Slowly Angel, Doyle, and Cordelia advanced toward the fire demon, keeping up their barrage. Angel could feel the heat, pulsing against his face in time to the rhythm of Feutoch's screams.

Then, as if somebody somewhere had thrown a switch, both the sound and the heat cut off. The sound of the extinguishers was the only one that he could hear.

"Stop!" Angel called.

Doyle dropped his extinguisher to the floor with a metal clang and ran to Terri Miller's side.

"Now I know what a Ghostbuster feels like," Cordelia said. "We got him, right?"

Waving away smoke and extinguisher fumes, Angel stared down. For a moment he could have sworn he saw all that remained of Deirdre and Tucker. Their bodies reduced to fine white ash. They were lying on the floor. Deirdre's head was tucked against Tucker's neck, as if he'd tried to shield her from the flames at the very last moment.

Then a gust of wind swirled in through the open warehouse door, and what had been the outline of two human figures became a pile of ash on a concrete floor.

Of Feutoch, there was no sign at all. Unless you counted scorch marks.

"Yeah," Angel said. "We got him."

Cordelia pursed her lips. "How come nobody tried that before?"

"Fire extinguishers probably hadn't been invented the last time Feutoch put in an appearance."

Angel turned to where Doyle was helping a shaky Terri Miller to her feet.

"Come on," he said. "Let's go."

CHAPTER TWENTY-TWO

"You're sure you'll be okay?" Doyle asked.

He and Terri were sitting in a coffee shop at LAX, waiting for her flight to be called.

"I think so." Terri nodded, her eyes on her coffee cup. She made a face. "I'll probably have nightmares for a while. And then there's the part where I'm finding it hard to forgive myself. But, hey—other than that . . ."

"You'll be okay," Doyle said. He was sorry about the nightmares, but lots of trauma victims had them. Not just those who'd gotten up close and personal with a fire-demon cult.

"Sometimes people . . . make mistakes."

Terri looked up quickly. "A mistake. Is that what you'd call what I did?"

"What else do you want me to call it? You don't need me to blame you, Terri," Doyle said. "Seems to me you're doing a bang-up job of that all by yourself. I know I promised never to give you more advice—"

"But your advice is—"

"Get over it. Not everybody gets a second chance."

Terri was quiet for a moment. "I know that. It's just—" She fell silent once more, her fingers toying with the handle of the coffee cup. "You aren't going to tell me, are you?"

"What?"

"You know," Terri said. "What really happened. With my eyes taped shut, I couldn't really—"

"You're right. I'm not going to tell you," Doyle interrupted. "If I thought it would help you get over this, I would."

"Sound a little more definite, why don't you?"

Doyle smiled. *Terri looks pretty good,* he thought. There was something about her that hadn't been there before. He thought it was a sense of self.

He took a sip of his own coffee. "So, Sacramento, huh?"

Terri laughed again. "Okay, I can take a hint. Shall we change the subject?" She pulled in a breath. "Yeah, Sacramento. I have an old school friend there. She needs a roommate, I need a new apartment. Plus, I did some checking. I'm thinking of applying to the college where my friend goes. She says they have a pretty good program if you want to go into some sort of social work."

"Social work?" Doyle's eyebrows rose. "Is this about that guy—"

"Septimus," Terri filled in. "In a way. I guess so. All this time I was feeling like nobody ever saw me, but people like Septimus, nobody *wants* to see them. He tried to save my life, Doyle. That's what your friend Angel said. But I still don't understand why. All I know is Septimus looked at me and saw something nobody else saw. But I hardly noticed him. People shouldn't live like he did. It's not right, Doyle."

She broke off, made a face. "I probably sound like some sort of naïve Pollyanna, don't I?"

"You sound like somebody who cares," Doyle said. "Doing social work isn't easy, you know."

"What difference does that make?" Terri asked. "Maybe, if I hadn't wanted an easy way out this time, I wouldn't have ended up . . . you know."

At the sound of a voice over the loudspeaker, Terri lifted her head. "That's it," she said. "They're calling my flight." She got to her feet. Doyle followed suit, picking up the suitcase that sat beside the table.

"This it?"

Terri flushed, then recovered by reaching to reclaim the suitcase. "Yep, that's it. Pathetic, I know. But I didn't want to take anything that didn't really belong to me, if you know what I mean."

"Personally, I think traveling light is an excellent idea," Doyle remarked.

Together, they walked to the gate. "I'm at the front of the plane," Terri said. "It'll be a few minutes still. You don't have to wait, if you don't want to."

"That's okay," Doyle answered.

They were silent for a moment, watching the other passengers file onto the jetway. Doyle could feel Terri fidgeting ever so slightly as she stood beside him.

"Doyle?"

"Hmmm?"

"There's still one thing I want to know. When you asked me out, were you . . . what I mean is, did you really . . . you weren't just—"

"Yes," Doyle said. "And no."

Terri expelled a breath.

"Yes, I really wanted to," Doyle said quietly. "No, I wasn't just being nice. It wasn't just a job."

Terri stood silently. From the corner of his eye Doyle could see her throat move as she swallowed.

"Thanks," she said. She fished in her purse, pulled out a tiny gold box of chocolates wrapped with a fancy bow. She thrust it into Doyle's hands.

"Somebody I know once told me any jerk

could buy a bag of M&M's. This is so you know I'm going to hold out for the good stuff this time around."

Before Doyle could respond, she walked off. He watched as she handed her boarding pass to the flight attendant and disappeared down the jetway, holding her single suitcase firmly in one hand.

"Have a nice life, Terri Miller," Doyle said.

Angel stood in the deep shade cast by an old oak tree, watching Kate as she stood at Deirdre's grave. Though the notion of a grave was mostly symbolic. There hadn't been much left of Deirdre to bury. But what there was now rested beside the grave of Martin Arensen, her father.

Her accomplice, and her victim, Angel thought. He knew that now.

Kate stood, unmoving. Her back ramrod straight. The last few days had to have been tough on her, Angel thought. With the deaths of Andrew Jackson Tucker and Deirdre Arensen, the Krispy Kritter killings had ceased as abruptly as they'd begun.

The press was indulging in a frenzy of speculation. Personal papers found among the effects of both the final victims strongly suggested they might have been something other than what they'd claimed. The press was calling it a death cult ending in a suicide pact.

Close enough, Angel thought. And the rest was something nobody else ever needed to know.

Kate knelt and placed a single white rose on Deirdre's grave. Then she got up, turned around. Angel knew the exact second she caught sight of him. She stopped short. Hesitated a moment. Then strode purposefully across the grass toward him. When she got to the oak, she stopped. She regarded him steadily, but Angel could see that her blue eyes were troubled.

"I'm sorry, Kate," he said.

Kate's expression tightened. "Don't apologize to me," she rapped out. "You don't have anything to be sorry for. Don't you read the papers? She brought this on herself. Hell, I should probably be apologizing to you. I brought her to you. I could have killed you all."

"You didn't."

"I thought I knew her!" Kate burst out. "Not every single detail, but enough to know I could believe in her. That she was someone I could trust. I've seen what they found in her—in Martin's—apartment. It's unbelievable—crazy stuff. I feel so used and stupid."

Join the club, Angel thought. He supposed the fact that he'd made the right decision in the end ought to make him feel better. It didn't. Not by much. It had been too close a call. If Tucker's accusations hadn't suddenly added up—if Deirdre hadn't all but admitted to being the Summoner when she'd bragged that Feutoch wouldn't kill her because he needed her, would Angel have made his biggest mistake of all and saved her life? He'd never know.

"Stop beating yourself up, Kate," he said now. "You did the best you could. That's all you can hope for. It's not your fault Deirdre wasn't what you thought she was. Nobody is. We all have things to hide."

"How do you hide something that big?" Kate asked.

"You'd be surprised."

Kate rubbed her forehead as if it hurt. "Apparently, you're right. Because I never saw this coming, Angel. I swear to God. Oh, for crying out loud, now what?" she barked as her pager went off. She pulled it from her purse, checked the number. "I'd better go. Duty calls."

"How are things at work these days?"

Kate gave a short, unamused laugh. "I'll tell you sometime. When I can spare a decade or so. Can I drop you somewhere?"

"No, thanks," Angel said. "I've got my car."

"Then I guess I'll see you around," Kate said.

"Right." The sun sank below the horizon as he watched her walk to her car. He waited until she'd driven off before he turned toward the convertible. Doyle and Cordelia were leaning against the driver's door.

"What are you, the welcoming committee?" he asked as he walked toward them.

"He's been brooding," Cordelia said. "I told you so."

"I do not brood."

"Since when?" Cordelia countered. "We know you, Angel. We've been watching you for days now. You're beating yourself up over the way you let Deirdre Arensen fool you. Us. We're here to tell you to knock it off."

Doyle nodded, his gesture backing up Cordelia's words.

"Besides," Cordy went on, "if anybody's going to do any beating, it's going to be us."

"That makes me feel so much better," Angel said.

Cordelia snorted. "Well, I should certainly hope so. I mean, I hate to say this, Angel, but you did come awfully close to screwing up."

"Thanks a lot."

"Fortunately for you," Cordelia continued blithely. "I've been doing some reading and I've come up with a solution. Team-building exercises."

"*What?*"

"It's these techniques to help you work well with others," Doyle explained. "Including basic concepts such as trusting your fellow teammates."

"*And* keeping them informed. You should have told us about the way Wolfram and Hart marked you, Angel," Cordelia said.

"I did tell you."

"Only when everything was all over. You should have told us when we could have helped."

"You couldn't have helped," Angel said. "That's why I didn't tell you."

"Okay, see, this is just the kind of thing I mean," Cordelia said. "This is why we need to do some team-building exercises. There's this club where you can go, have dinner and drinks, and play these games. They're supposed to establish rapport."

"We have rapport," Angel said. "I'm the boss. You do what I tell you."

Doyle shot Cordelia a look. "He has a point."

"Teams have leaders, Cordelia," Angel went on. "This isn't a democracy. Sometimes, I have to make choices."

"Okay, fine," Cordelia said, her tone of voice saying she hadn't quite given up. "But how about next time you *choose* to keep us informed? You're supposed to let us help you, Angel. It's part of the deal, remember? I think the PTBs would want it that way."

"Okay," Angel said. "I'll try." He opened the car door, slid behind the wheel. "Any word on Septimus?" he asked as Doyle slid in on the passenger side. Cordelia climbed into the back.

"Not a thing," Doyle said. "He just walked right out of the hospital and vanished into thin air. I'll keep my ear to the ground, though. He'll surface somewhere, sooner or later."

No, he won't, Angel thought. He'd seen guys like Septimus all his life, and particularly after. They were the forgotten ones.

"Speaking of ears," Cordelia said. She leaned forward to peer over Doyle's shoulder as Angel started the car. "Shouldn't you be feeling a headache coming on right about now?"

"What does that have to do with ears?" Doyle asked.

"Well, they're on your head, aren't they?" Cordelia inquired. "I hate to pressure you or anything, but we do rely on you to keep us in business. We never saw any money from that last gig, you know."

"It doesn't feel so good right now," Doyle muttered darkly.

Cordelia brightened instantly. "Really? Not so good in a regular way, or not so good in a vision way?"

Angel pulled away from the curb, heading for home.

Through the night Septimus Stephens walked the streets, just as he'd done all the other nights since he'd left the hospital. He knew Terri's new friends, those who'd really been the ones to save her, had wanted him to stay there. But Septimus couldn't do that. It was too exposed. Besides, he hardly felt the pain in his shoulder at all anymore. And even when he did, it hardly compared with the pain in his heart.

He was alone now. Terri was gone.

During the day, he told himself that he was glad. She'd never really belonged here. She would be happier somewhere else. Septimus stayed still during the day now. It was only when the shadows started to lengthen, when night began to fall, that he grew restless. That the pain would return. That was when he began to walk. Only by movement could he keep the terrible truth at bay.

Terri had been saved, but he had not been the one to save her. His punishment would be to always be alone.

At least he had a token. One thing to remember her by. He'd scooped it up from the floor of the warehouse right after he'd regained consciousness. Right before Terri's new friends had helped him out the door. He'd liked them, but he hadn't shown the thing he'd found to anyone. Showing your treasures meant someone could come to take them away.

Thrusting his hand into the pocket of his overcoat, Septimus turned over and over between his fingers the thing that looked like an old coin.